"He's so quiet.

"The kid's just been dumped with a stranger. He'll warm to you," Ben insisted.

Olivia shook her head. "I don't know anything about being a mom, and what about all the work coming up with the bicentennial?"

Ben touched her chin with his fingertip. "It'll be all right. I'll be right here to help."

Even Ben's reassuring words couldn't stop the rising panic in her chest. "This isn't going to work."

"We'll make it work. For the little guy. He needs us, Livvy. He doesn't have anyone else."

"I don't know what to do."

"But I do. My brother Jeff has three kids. I stayed with him when I got back from…a while back. Don't worry. We'll face this together. I'd better check on the little man."

Olivia watched him put more cookies on the plate, which earned him a small smile from her nephew. Her fears slowly ebbed as she watched the pair. Ben's assurance of help was profoundly reassuring.

She had one more item to add to her Good list.

Rescuer.

Lorraine Beatty was raised in Columbus, Ohio, but now calls Mississippi home. She and her husband, Joe, have two sons and five grandchildren. Lorraine started writing in junior high and is a member of RWA and ACFW, and is a charter member and past president of Magnolia State Romance Writers. In her spare time she likes to work in her garden, travel and spend time with her family.

Books by Lorraine Beatty

Love Inspired

The Orphans' Blessing
Her Secret Hope
The Family He Needs
The Loner's Secret Past
The Widow's Choice
The Guardian Agreement

Mississippi Hearts

Her Fresh Start Family
Their Family Legacy
Their Family Blessing

Visit the Author Profile page at LoveInspired.com for more titles.

The Guardian Agreement

Lorraine Beatty

LOVE INSPIRED
INSPIRATIONAL ROMANCE

LOVE INSPIRED®

INSPIRATIONAL ROMANCE

Recycling programs
for this product may
not exist in your area.

ISBN-13: 978-1-335-59856-1

The Guardian Agreement

Copyright © 2023 by Lorraine Beatty

For questions and comments about the quality of this book, please contact us at CustomerService@Harlequin.com.

Love Inspired
22 Adelaide St. West, 41st Floor
Toronto, Ontario M5H 4E3, Canada
www.LoveInspired.com

Printed in U.S.A.

Nay, in all these things we are more than conquerors through him that loved us.
                              —*Romans* 8:37

To Joe, my precious hubby of fifty-five years. Truly the love of my life.

Chapter One

Olivia Marshall dropped her leather satchel, purse and lunch bag onto her desk and sank into the cushioned chair. Her gaze landed on the calendar, and she huffed out a heavy sigh. The Blessing, Mississippi Bicentennial was only a few weeks away and once it was over, she'd be able to take a long-needed vacation. The last year had been filled with one event after the other, all building to the big day at the end of April. Her job as bicentennial liaison coordinator had been exciting and fulfilling, but she was more than ready for a break.

Her boss had handed her one last project, overseeing the design and assembly of a special souvenir booklet highlighting the two hundredth birthday celebrations, and she was looking forward to the challenge. She'd held many jobs with the committee for the last three years, but this one was the most exciting. Her baby. Her design and her vision. Most importantly, it would give a boost to her résumé when she applied for the town manager job later this spring.

She leaned back in her chair. Only one slight problem. She had to find a photographer to help her document the dozens of events surrounding the big day. The last one had resigned for a better position. She couldn't blame the woman, but it had left Olivia in limbo.

"Olivia, I have good news."

Olivia glanced up as her boss entered her office. Delores Porter was the director of the bicentennial committee and had hired Olivia three years ago when the committee was first organized to plan the two hundredth birthday event.

She smiled and tapped the desktop. "I've found you a photographer."

"That was fast. Justine only quit last week. Can they start right away? I don't want to get any further behind on this job than I already am. It's going to be hectic trying to document and photograph all the events coming up."

Delores held up a hand. "No problem. He can start right away and he has good credentials. He's in my office. You want me to send him in to see you?"

"That's fine. I'll fill him in. I just hope he's as good as you claim."

"Oh, and there's a change in plans today. I want you to go to the history museum. The chairman of the city quilt committee has decided the quilt should be displayed in the new museum building since the quilt represents the history of the town."

"Sounds good. I'll rearrange a couple of things, then get on it." Olivia turned her attention to her schedule and adjusted for the changes. She was vaguely aware of someone entering her small office; she glanced up and froze. Her mind rejected what she was seeing. Her heart turned to ice in her chest. Heat surged up through her ribs and into her neck, tightening her throat and making it hard to breathe.

Ben! Why was Ben Kincaid in her office? She never wanted to see him again ever.

"Hello, Olivia. It's good to see you."

The memory of his raspy voice sliced through her nerves and unleashed an anger that she'd believed she'd conquered a long time ago. She clenched her teeth and glared at the tall handsome man in front of her.

"Get out. I have nothing to say to you."

He inhaled a slow breath and shrugged. "I can't. I'm your new photographer."

She could only stare in shock. "No. No, you're not." Was Delores serious? There was no way she could work with the man who had left her dressed in her wedding gown, ready to walk down the aisle, then sent a note saying he wasn't coming.

Anger flooded her senses. She stood and walked out of her office, catching a whiff of the aftershave he'd favored as she passed him. The memory lanced through her like a hot sword. She struggled to control the pain.

Olivia stormed into Delores's office. "I can't work with this man. You'll have to find someone else."

Delores swung around in her chair and frowned. "Why would I do that? He's perfect."

Perfectly unsuitable. "I…know him. We can't get along."

Delores raised her brows and removed her glasses. "Well, I'm sorry, but you have no choice. He's the only one available right now. May I remind you we are on a very tight timeline? I suggest you find a way to work this out."

Olivia's stomach twisted into a knot. "You

don't understand. He's my former fiancé." Saying the words sent a sting to her heart.

Delores made a dismissive gesture. "Then you should be able to find a way to team up."

"No. He…" She didn't want to tell her boss the truth. It was too humiliating, too painful. It had taken her three years of hard work to overcome being jilted. "He left me at the altar."

Delores looked up with the pitiful expression Olivia had come to despise. "Oh, he's the one, huh? Well, I'm sorry—I really am. I can't imagine how difficult this must be, but we have no choice. I'll look around for someone else, but the only option at the moment is a high school kid. In the meantime you need to set aside the past and do your job. We need to get this booklet to the printer as soon after the bicentennial celebration is over as possible."

Olivia had worked for the woman a long time and she knew the tone of her voice meant her decision was final. She was not going to give in. Returning to her office, Olivia hoped Ben had left, but he was looking out the window, his back to her. He'd crossed his arms over his chest, making the material of his knit shirt stretch across his broad shoulders. She tried to squash the rush of appreciation that flowed through her without warning.

She gritted her teeth and dug down to find her work persona, the one that had carried her through the last three years.

"Why are you here?"

He turned slowly and met her gaze. He didn't smile. Odd. Ben was always smiling and always flirting, making use of his dimples and his dreamy blue eyes. She raised her chin. She'd succumbed to his good looks and skillful charm once. Never again.

"I wanted to see you…again."

"Why? Just to gloat?" She hadn't meant to swipe at him, but she was barely holding it together.

"No, Olivia, I'd never do that."

"I used to think there were a lot of things you'd never do. I was wrong." She went and stood behind her desk, trying to ignore the way his blue shirt brought out those blue eyes. "Why did you take this job?"

"I needed the money."

Olivia nearly laughed out loud. "Right. The rich playboy needs money so you get a job as a photographer for a small-town celebration. What do you know about taking pictures?" Ben took a step toward her and she moved away.

"I know a lot. I've always been interested

in photography. I was a sports photographer in college, remember?"

"No. I don't. You never told me that."

Delores entered the office. "Olivia, Edwina Cole called from the museum. They are nearly ready to hang the quilt. I want pictures of that. You'd better get going."

Olivia's nerves chilled and vibrated with emotion. How was she going to do this? How could she work with Ben when all she wanted to do was make him disappear? Forever. A small voice reminded her that she was in charge here. This was her job, her area of expertise. Ben was just the guy with the camera.

Grabbing up her satchel and purse, she started from the room. "Meet me at St. Joseph's Church, ASAP."

Ben hurried after her. "Shouldn't we go together?"

She stopped in her tracks, turned around and looked him in the eyes. "Ab-so-lute-ly not." Satisfied at the shock reflected in his face, she marched out and didn't allow herself to think or breathe until she was safely locked in her car.

Alone and secure, her emotions spilled over, and she gulped in a deep breath and exhaled a sob. All the anger and hurt from her shattered wedding day rose up from the crypt she'd sealed them in. Gripping the steering wheel, she fought them back. She'd gotten good at it over the years. She would not, could not, work with Ben Kincaid. If that meant quitting her job then that's what she would do. Her heart couldn't survive his presence. Not a second time.

Pushing the ignition button, she drove out of the parking lot and headed for the newly acquired Blessing History Museum, wishing Ben would get lost on the way and never show up.

Ben Kincaid watched Olivia storm off, realizing he'd greatly underestimated her reaction to his return. He'd anticipated anger, tears and even a sock on the jaw as a possibility. He'd been under the notion that three years might have eased her feelings about what he'd done. Obviously, he had been wrong.

He hadn't been prepared for the pain in her brown eyes, or the hurt in her voice. Coming here might have been a mistake, but he wasn't going to give up after their first meeting. A wave of guilt engulfed him. He was responsible for that pain in her eyes, the hurt in her voice, and it was up to him to try and ease that somehow. He had so much to make up for. Not only to Olivia but others as well. His sense of failure started to expand.

After reaching into his pocket, he pulled out a peppermint, unwrapped it and popped it in his mouth. The sweet taste took his mind off the emotion trying to overtake him.

He needed to catch up with Olivia. After stopping by Delores's office for directions, he headed out, hoping he didn't get lost. Olivia would be furious if he messed up on his first job. He wasn't from Blessing. It had been Olivia's desire to be married in one of the small town's historic old churches. He'd wanted to run off to Vegas. He winced at the thought. It sounded so cheesy to him now. Olivia deserved a proper church wedding. Why hadn't he seen that before?

Ben found the church with little trouble; the large sign in the front yard declaring it as the history museum had helped. Quickly he pulled out his camera and headed inside. Olivia was talking to a tall redheaded woman across the room. Two men were lifting the framed quilt onto the braces on the wall. He had no idea what the significance of the quilt might be, but he'd figure it out. All he wanted now was to get as many shots as possible. He scanned the room through the lens and snapped some activity in the corner. When he focused on the quilt again Olivia was standing in front of it, one hand lightly touching one of the many small colorful squares that formed the coverlet. The expression on her face caught his breath. She looked so lovely, so translucent he couldn't take his eyes off her. Her wavy brown hair caressed her neck gently, its rich color highlighted by the pink blouse she wore.

He tried to discern her expression but failed to find the right word. She looked proud, sad and moved all at the same time. He vowed to ask her about it if he ever got the chance. As if reading his mind, she turned and faced him. His heart jumped. Forcing a smile, he went toward her. He'd forgotten how lovely she was and how easily she could affect him.

"I've got shots of the quilt being hung in place. What else do you want?"

She looked away. "That should be enough."

The red-headed woman came toward him. "I'd like pictures of the quilt up close, maybe some from a lower angle. I have a project I want to do. Hello, I'm Edwina Cole."

Ben lowered his camera and shook her hand. "Ben Kincaid." He glanced around. "Is this a new museum?" The space was sparsely filled.

Edwina smiled. "As a matter of fact, it is.

A local businessman had created a private museum here, but decided it would be better served in the hands of the historical society and donated the building. We're trying to get a few special items displayed for the celebration. It'll take longer to make this a full-fledged museum."

Ben nodded. "Interesting. I'd like to get shots of you with the quilt if you don't mind. It'll add a personal touch."

Ben didn't realize how long he'd been working until Olivia cleared her throat. "Are you finished?"

"Oh, yeah. Sure." He thanked Edwina then followed Olivia out to the parking lot. He took shots of the old church before facing her. "So, what's the story behind the quilt? Someone important make it?" She kept her gaze averted when she replied.

"Many someones. It's a community quilt. Nearly every family contributed. Some of those squares are from clothing that's hundreds of years old, others from current families. It's a beautiful representation of the history of our town."

Ben smiled. "That's nice. A great story. Are you going to caption the picture with that explanation?"

"I don't know. I'll decide when I see the photos."

Ben slipped his camera into its case. "Well, if I was buying one of these booklets, I'd want a little info for each photo to jog my memory. Sometimes a picture alone isn't enough."

Olivia stared at him a moment then pulled out her phone. "I need your number."

Ben raised his eyebrows. "Sure. Where to next?"

"Nowhere. I'm going back to the office to handle an issue Edwina has. I'll call you if there's something else I need photographed. I assume you're staying someplace in town?"

"Uh, yes. I can report for duty at the drop of a hat. No worries."

She turned away and reached for the door handle of her car. He didn't want her to leave. He had so much he wanted to say. "Livvy, we need to talk."

She whirled around, her brown eyes dark. "Don't call me that. My name is Olivia. And there's nothing we need to talk about."

"Please, Olivia, if you'd just give me a few minutes."

"I was ready to give you my future but that wasn't good enough." She shrugged. "There's nothing else to say."

Ben watched with a knot in his stomach

as she got in the car and drove off. What a fool he was. He'd convinced himself that if he could just talk to her, explain what he'd been thinking that day, she'd at least understand. His only hope now was that spending time together would start to break down her wall enough for him to tell her how sorry he was.

Inside his SUV, he emailed his photos to Olivia then stared out the window at the old church. It wasn't the one they were supposed to have been married in, but it took his thoughts back to that day. Their wedding day. The day he realized just how much he loved her and how wrong he was for her.

Today he realized that despite the passage of time, and all the changes in his life, he was still completely, hopelessly in love with Olivia Marshall.

Delores called to her the moment she entered the office. Olivia hadn't returned after the museum shoot was completed. She'd driven to the coffee shop, ordered her favorite brew and parked in the shade of a tree on the square. The flavored coffee only partially distracted her thoughts from Ben. There was no way she could dismiss him completely. Seeing him again, having to be close to him daily, was like pouring acid on a partially healed scar.

Yet, the ugly truth was, being near Ben had unleashed all her old feelings for him and on top of the pile was the fact that she still *had* feelings for him. What kind of masochist did that make her? The man humiliated her in front of the whole town, cut her heart out of her body, and left her dead and empty, and yet she looked at him now and felt the old stirrings.

Emotional muscle memory. That's all it was. Not real, sincere affection.

Olivia entered her boss's office, hoping she'd found another photographer. Delores didn't give her a moment to speak. "Have you seen these?" She spun her computer screen around to display the pictures Ben had taken. "These are amazing. He has a real eye for this. He even suggested we add the personal touch by mentioning the reason behind the quilt project and the new museum." Delores smiled. "We have a real winner in this guy."

Olivia set her jaw. "If you say so."

Her boss eyed her closely. "Oh, didn't it go well? You and the ex I mean."

Olivia had never felt so trapped. There was no convenient answer. Either way she responded she'd still have to work with Ben.

It was a no-win situation. "It was fine. He did his job. I did mine."

"Good. Olivia, it's only for a few weeks. Just shut down your emotions and get through it. That's what I do." Delores smiled. "Think about how much you've accomplished since you came here and how much you've changed. Don't give that up for a short-term partnership that'll be over soon."

Olivia nodded. She knew her boss meant well. "I'll work from home the rest of the day if you don't mind."

"Sure. See you tomorrow."

Safely in her small bungalow home, Olivia fixed a glass of tea and curled up on the sofa, her gaze scanning her cozy living room. Her new house was perfect. She'd lovingly selected each piece of furniture, each rug, lamp and wall hanging, to suit her taste. When she stepped inside the room, her tension dropped, her mood lifted and she felt a sense of contentment she'd rarely experienced in her life.

Except for today. Instead of feeling relaxed she was edgy and tense.

She'd worked hard to put her life back together after that fateful day. She'd gone to work for the bicentennial committee, bought her own home, buried all memories of the pain and humiliation. And Ben. She'd proved to herself that she was capable, resilient and strong. She could rise above anything life could throw at her. But how did she get through Ben showing up in her world again?

He wanted to talk? Was he out of his mind? Nothing he could say would erase the pain of that day. Even now, she could feel the emotions that had slammed into her as she sat in her wedding gown, veil draped over her shoulders, bouquet within reach, and learned that he wasn't coming. He didn't love her enough to spend his life with her. He'd chosen freedom over commitment. It was as if all the scaffolding holding her together had collapsed and she was sitting in a pile of debris trying to dig her way out.

Why was he really back? There had to be a reason other than wanting to talk.

A low groan escaped her lips at the knock on the door. She really didn't want to see anyone. Before she could move, the door opened, and her good friend and coworker Marcy Jo Conner peeked in. "Oh, it's you. Come on in."

Marcy Jo had been the first friend she'd made when she moved to Blessing in high school, and they had remained close ever since. Marcy Jo was supposed to have been her maid of honor.

"Hey, Ollie, I wanted to check on you. I heard about what's-his-name coming back."

Marcy Jo was the only person on the planet who could call her by such a silly name. Olivia shook her head. "I can't believe he's here or why in the world he would come back, let alone take a job working with me."

Marcy Jo curled up at the other end of the sofa. "I have no idea. After what he did, I'd think he would want to stay as far away as possible. Did he say why he's here?"

"He said he wants to talk about what happened." Olivia snorted. "I don't think so."

"How did it go today? Delores told me he went with you to the museum."

She shrugged and picked at the fringe on the sofa pillow. "Fine. I simply shut down my emotions and did my job and he did his."

"Well, that's good." She stood and headed toward the kitchen. "Mind if I get a cool drink? Still, it must have been hard for you."

"I'm over him. Have been for a long time. I'm a different person now." Marcy Jo returned and met her gaze.

"And what about him? Has he changed much?"

Olivia started to say no but paused. "Actually, now that I think about it, he was different. He was usually so smiley and flirty all the time. He was always making jokes, having fun and never taking anything seriously. But he was quiet today. Serious. The only time I saw him smile was when he met Edwina at the museum."

Marcy Jo set her drink on a coaster. "Maybe he grew up. They say men mature later than women do."

She went over their brief conversations. "He said he needed the money. That's why he took the job."

Marcy Jo frowned. "Uh, excuse me, there are better-paying jobs he could have found that weren't in Blessing working with you."

"I know. I hope he doesn't have any ideas about us getting together again. That'll never happen."

Marcy Jo pulled her knees up. "No way, though I caught sight of him as I was leaving the office. He was meeting with Delores. He hasn't lost his looks. If anything, he's aged very well." Marcy Jo grimaced, obviously regretting her comment. "Sorry, but he always was a looker. You two were a beautiful couple."

"It takes more than good looks to make a relationship. Ben didn't have what it takes to make a commitment." She couldn't deny the years had been kind to him. There were small lines at the corners of his sky-blue eyes; his physique was more muscular than she remembered, the shoulders more broad. The dimples still winked when he spoke.

"I wonder what he's been doing all this time"

Olivia had wondered the same thing briefly. "Don't know and don't care." Despite her words, there had been something different about Ben she couldn't dismiss. She'd seen it in his eyes, but she'd been afraid to look too deep because her mind and her heart were at war, and she had a bad feeling she was in for an emotional tug-of-war over the next several weeks. What was it the pastor had said last week? Something about guarding your heart for the heart was "deceitful above all things."

She knew firsthand that it was a true statement. Her heart had told her lies about Ben. From now on she'd be on alert and put on her shield and keep the old attraction and responses behind it. Ben was just a man taking pictures. Nothing more.

Ben stopped his SUV in the alleyway behind the large craftsman house and gathered up his equipment. His mind was a seesaw of thoughts and impressions. He had no idea where to start sorting through them. The scenario he'd envisioned in his mind upon meeting Olivia again had borne no resemblance to the events that had actually played out.

He stepped into the cozy kitchen and inhaled the aroma of roast beef and noodles. Aunt Nora must have sensed he'd need comfort food tonight. If it wasn't for his dad's sister, Ben wouldn't be working with Olivia or in Blessing at all. Not only had she offered him a place to stay, but she'd told him about the opening with Olivia and pulled a couple strings to get him the job.

"There you are. How did it go today?"

Ben answered with a sour glance.

"Ah. Well, I'm not surprised." She reached out and took his chin in her hand, turning his face from one side to the other. "I don't see any red marks or scars, so I guess she didn't get violent."

Ben smiled and shook his head. "No. Olivia's not that type."

Nora peered at him over the rim of her glasses. "You leave a bride at the altar, she becomes a different type. Mark my words."

Ben hoped she was wrong. He'd liked Olivia the way he remembered her. Sweet, happy, delighted with new experiences. And loving.

"Will you be going back tomorrow?"

Ben set his camera bag at the end of the counter. "Yes. The boss really liked the work I did today."

"That's good. What did Olivia think?"

"Not sure. We didn't actually talk much."

"Give her time, Ben. Be patient. You hurt her deeply. That's not something a woman can get over easily. If ever."

The thought was depressing. "It was three years ago."

Nora frowned. "It was her wedding day. You didn't have sisters, so you don't understand what a wedding means to a girl. Some start planning it when they're in grade school. Every detail is important. The napkins, the font on the invitations, the cake decorations, the color of the flowers. When it doesn't happen—all those dreams, all those years of seeing herself as a princess, the focus of attention, dressed in a gown she'll never wear again—she's not simply disappointed, she's shattered into a thousand pieces." She pointed a finger at him. "And sometimes those pieces can't ever be put together again."

Ben ran a hand over his head. "Thanks, Aunt Nora, that makes me feel a whole lot better."

"Sorry, but you need to tread carefully and be extra kind and understanding. This isn't just getting in touch with an old flame, you know."

"I know. At least, I thought I did. I'm not so sure anymore."

"Are you sure this plan of yours is necessary?"

He nodded. "I can't move forward with my life until I find some closure with Olivia. The guilt gets heavier every day."

His aunt sighed. "Tell me—is talking to Olivia all you want?"

He couldn't honestly answer yes. Yesterday he'd been positive of his reasons for coming to Blessing; now, after seeing Olivia again, being near her, he knew his heart was still held in her hand. "It's all I can expect."

Nora reached out and laid her hand on his. "What about you, Ben? Are you going to be able to handle this? Are you strong enough? I don't want you being overwhelmed and falling back into that dark place again."

"I won't. I got the all clear from my doctor and I'm well equipped to handle anything that comes up. Promise. Don't worry."

"I was never sure of your reason for walking out on the wedding. Did you get cold feet?"

Ben shook his head and studied his hands. He wasn't ready to share the details. He was saving that for Olivia's ears only. "No. I realized that all I really wanted was for Olivia to be happy and I knew I wasn't the one to do that."

"You didn't know that for certain."

"I did. I had no idea how to be a good husband and be faithful to one woman. Dad is working on wife number five. Mom was always gone on her latest new age retreat. I wanted to give Olivia a real marriage, but I had no idea how to do that."

"I'll pray that you and she can find a common meeting place."

As usual Aunt Nora's meal was perfection and Ben left the kitchen satisfied and waiting for the cookies she promised to bake a little later. The living room was quiet and comfortable with a wide front window that looked out at the light blue bungalow across the street. Olivia's house. Her car was parked at the curb in front, and the lights from inside gave the little home an inviting appearance. He'd like to be inside, sitting with her, going over the day's events, but it was a dream he shouldn't encourage.

He thought about what Nora had told him. He knew leaving Olivia on their wedding day was a cruel thing to do, but had he underestimated how deeply he'd hurt her?

He sensed his aunt enter the room.

"I see you parked in the back of the house. When will you tell her that you live across the street?"

Ben turned away. "When the time is right."

She placed a plate of warm cookies on the coffee table. "Kiddo, the time is never right."

He had a feeling her words held more truth than either realized. There was so much he wanted to tell Olivia, but he doubted if the right time would ever come. Not a second time. He'd lost the right to hope for that three years ago.

Chapter Two

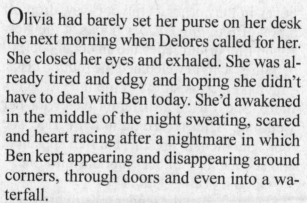

Olivia had barely set her purse on her desk the next morning when Delores called for her. She closed her eyes and exhaled. She was already tired and edgy and hoping she didn't have to deal with Ben today. She'd awakened in the middle of the night sweating, scared and heart racing after a nightmare in which Ben kept appearing and disappearing around corners, through doors and even into a waterfall.

It didn't take a psychologist to interpret those dreams. She was terrified that Ben would walk out on the job the way he walked out on their wedding. Part of her wished he would. Another part realized she needed his skills to complete this booklet project and give her the edge on the town manager job. She had to think of her future. Something her mother had drilled into her from an early age. *"Men can't be counted on, Olivia. They'll let you down every time."* As much as she hated to admit it, her mother had been right on that.

Delores looked up when she approached her desk. "I got a call from Mona at Blair's Bakery. She wants you to come and photograph her design for the commemorative dessert. She also has questions about the presentation." She motioned toward a stack of boxes in the corner. "On your way, drop off a box of *Blessing History* books at the New Again Emporium. They are all out of copies."

"Sure." Olivia welcomed the routine tasks. The bakery was safe. No memory triggers there. She'd used a different baker for her wedding. After returning to her office, she took a moment to breathe, but Ben appeared, and she had to pull her emotions into line.

"Good morning, Olivia."

She winced at the tender tone in his voice. It brought to mind a picnic under a fall tree that rained down golden leaves. She bit her lip to shut down the memory. Shield firmly in place, she stood. "We need to go. I have a delivery to make then we have to meet with Mona at the bakery."

Ben grinned, flashing both dimples. "I'm ready."

Her heart skipped a beat. A surge of resentment crawled up inside her. Delores had already fallen prey to Ben's easy charm. Something she would never do again.

"Where should I meet you?"

She'd come to the realization last night that trying to avoid Ben and keep him at a distance physically might not be a good idea. Keeping her enemy close was a better plan. She needed to know where he was every minute to make sure he showed up and did his job.

Olivia climbed into her vehicle and started the engine. Ben rode beside her in the car. "What are we taking pictures of at the bakery?"

Olivia pulled to a stop in one of the angled parking slots on the town square. "Dessert." She knew she was being snotty, but she couldn't be a tolerant, noble person every minute. She got out and opened the back door and picked up the box.

"Hey, I'll get that." Ben reached for the door handle.

Olivia set her jaw. "I've got it. It's not heavy. I'll be right back."

When she returned to the car, she motioned for Ben to join her on the sidewalk.

"What's next? I think you said something

about a dessert? I've never shot a special pastry before."

Olivia studied him a moment. He was trying to scatter his charm around again. She wasn't susceptible to that anymore. "We can walk from here. Blair's Bakery is across the square."

She was painfully aware of Ben at her side and how he shortened his stride to match hers. The blue-and-red-plaid shirt gave him a rugged vibe that had always appealed to her. Her mind had so many memories of them walking these streets, holding hands and laughing. Tension hovered between them. Was he remembering too? She was relieved when Ben finally spoke.

"What kind of dessert am I shooting?"

"A cupcake."

"You're not serious."

Olivia knew how it must sound to him, but she wasn't about to let him make fun of such an important event. "Deadly. All of the shops have created special products during the last year to honor the birthday."

He chuckled. "So, there's a special ice-cream cone, and coffee blend and sandwich?"

His mocking tone fueled her irritation. She stopped and faced him. "Yes. It's a very important occasion." He looked appropriately apologetic.

"I'll keep that in mind."

They crossed the street and stopped at a charming storefront with a striped awning. The sign read Blair's Bakery.

Ben opened the door for her, and she breezed in. She was perfectly capable of opening her own doors, but it was something Ben had been very good at. Being a gentleman.

The bakery was nearly empty when they walked in, and Olivia started toward the kitchen to look for Mona. She stopped in her tracks when she saw the display counter. "Oh my. This is amazing."

Mona Blair entered, wiping her hands on her apron. "I was hoping you'd approve. Do you think it will be a fitting tribute to our birthday?"

Olivia smiled. "Oh yes." The large cupcake had a small Blessing Bridge perched on the top.

Ben leaned over the confection. "A bridge?"

"Yes, for the Blessing Bridge. It's spectacular. Ben, take a lot of pictures. This is so cool."

Ben got to work while Olivia chatted with Mona. "You are going to be famous for that design. It'll be the hit of the celebration."

Mona blushed. "Oh, I don't know about that, but I do hope people will enjoy it. It's chocolate cake with a mint cream cheese icing."

"Sounds yummy."

Olivia took Mona's arm. "Delores said you had something else you wanted to talk about?"

"Yes. Let's go back into the workshop and I'll explain."

Olivia glanced over her shoulder at Ben, but he was busy taking shots of the cupcake from every conceivable angle. At least she didn't have to be concerned about his work. He was good and thorough.

Ben watched Olivia walk away, aware of the difference in her since he'd seen her last. He'd forgotten how graceful she was, but now there was an air of confidence about her that hadn't been there before. The childlike enthusiasm he'd fallen in love with was gone, and in its place was a more serious, capable woman. He wondered if that fun-loving, filled-with-wonder person still existed. What had caused the change? The answer came to him with a hot sting. He had. Another consequence he'd never considered at the time.

But there were things about her that hadn't changed. Like the way her shoulder-length hair swished around her neck. It was cut in a more sophisticated style, but he had a feeling the texture was as silky as he remembered. Her smile still had the ability to light up a room, though it hadn't been directed at him so far. Maybe, if he got the opportunity, he'd discover a little of the Olivia he loved beneath her now unyielding demeanor.

If not, then he had another shovelful of guilt to add to his already large pile, and he wasn't sure how he'd deal with that.

"Ben."

He joined Olivia in the workroom. She and Mona were huddled over the desk in the corner. He took photos of the work area, but the space was small and windowless and he grew edgy. "I'll wait for you outside."

He pushed through the back door and found himself on a side street. He inhaled deeply several times then swung his camera over his shoulder. He glanced across the narrow way and saw an old building; its side door was chained and locked. Beside it a section of iron grillwork leaned against the wall.

His heart lurched inside his chest. His mouth went dry, and his thoughts soared backward. Fear paralyzed his muscles. A small voice called to him to pull away, to draw on his faith and counseling to regain his senses. He pulled out a peppermint from his pocket, unwrapped it and put it in his mouth.

"Ben."

He vaguely heard Olivia call his name, but he was powerless to respond, even as he fought to shut down the images swirling in his mind.

"Ben. What is it?"

He squinted. Her voice was getting closer. He needed to move and turn off the visions in his head.

"Ben!"

He felt her nudge his shoulder and blinked. The images vanished and he was looking again at the chained door and the grillwork. He braced, rubbed his eyes and glanced at Olivia. He was in Blessing, with Olivia, not in the mountains of Europe with Davey.

Her expression was filled with concern, her brown eyes probing.

"Are you all right? What's wrong?"

He forced a smile, at least he thought he did, and waved off her concern. "It's nothing. Just the beginnings of a migraine. Sorry. I never know when they're going to hit."

"I didn't know you had migraines."

"Yeah. For a long while." He didn't like lying to her, but he wasn't about to explain what had just happened. He may never be ready. She could never understand.

"Are you sure?"

"Right as rain." He could tell she didn't believe him or his explanation, but it couldn't be helped. Hopefully, she'd forget about it.

The way she'd forgotten about him.

Olivia glanced at Ben as they started back toward the car. He seemed fine now, but she had questions. Something was different about him; he was quiet and withdrawn as if he was protecting himself from something. Other times he was like she remembered. Lighthearted and cheerful.

Olivia waited in silence for the pedestrian light to change. She sensed Ben wanted to say something, but she wasn't going to engage in private conversation. She had work to do.

Ben scanned the photos on his camera. "How did she manage to make such a small bridge fit on that cupcake?"

"Mona is incredibly talented. She's made tiny houses, and animals and all kinds of things to top off her cakes and cookies."

Ben slipped his camera into its case. "No argument there. So, what's your special talent?"

She glanced over at him. Was he being sarcastic? His blue eyes looked sincere. "I don't have one."

When the walk signal flashed, she started across the street, not waiting for him. It took him a few seconds to catch up. They started down the street toward the car.

"You have a way with people, Olivia. That's a kind of talent."

She wasn't sure how to respond to that. But then, Ben had always been adept at saying the perfect thing at the perfect time to make you feel special. Ben must have sensed her withdrawal because he didn't speak again until they were in her vehicle.

"What's this Blessing Bridge you were talking about?"

Olivia shook her head inwardly. "You're kidding, right?"

"No. I never heard of it."

"It's our city landmark. Haven't you noticed the logo all over town?" She waved a hand in the direction of the courthouse in the center of downtown. The ironwork fencing, and arches, all displayed the image of the bridge. "We were supposed to have our wedding pictures taken there." Her cheeks flamed. Why had she said that? Why couldn't she keep those memories buried?

Ben spoke softly as they sat in the car. "I didn't remember that."

Heart aching, she bit back the harsh remark on the tip of her tongue. "Well, they say memory is the first thing to go."

Back at the office, they went their separate ways and Olivia was grateful for the space, though she had trouble keeping her mind on her work. She kept going over the morning with Ben. She couldn't make sense of his strange behavior at the bakery. He'd been taking pictures in the back room then suddenly walked out. When she joined him only minutes later he was staring into the distance. She'd had to nudge him to get a response. His explanation of a headache hadn't been convincing. She'd wracked her brain trying to remember him having one during the time they were together. No. It didn't fit.

After picking up her phone, she called Marcy Jo. Her friend battled migraines often and she'd know the signs. However, when she ended the call, she was more confused than ever. Ben's behavior bore no resemblance to the symptoms Marcy Jo had described. Of course, everyone was unique. Maybe Ben's headaches manifested themselves differently.

Still, she couldn't shake the feeling that something was going on with Ben. More importantly, why was he back? What did he want? What did he expect from her and what did he hope to gain? She could think of no reason for him to suddenly track her down after all this time.

Olivia checked the time. And where was he? He should have been back in the office by now. *He's gone.* The thought sprung into her mind unbidden. She rubbed her forehead. Her knee-jerk reaction was probably understandable, but was it fair?

Ben made an appearance a short while later with a rather sheepish look on his face. "Sorry. I've been with Delores. She'd like you to show me the photos of the main events from the last year to see which ones we can use in the booklet."

"I know." She'd already discussed it with her boss. She gestured Ben to the other computer in her office. "They should be on that one. Your predecessor used it."

Ben got to work, and Olivia tried to ignore him, which was not as easy as she'd hoped. There was a compelling energy about him that was impossible to dismiss. Her email alert sounded and she opened it to find a new file from Ben. He'd selected several photos for her to look at. He'd added a big question mark at the end.

She glanced over at him and found him studying her. His blue eyes held a twinkle she knew only too well. They did that when he was teasing her. It was his subtle way of pointing out how silly it was to email across the room. He was right, but sharing a screen together was too intimate and unsettling.

She slipped behind her professional facade. "Why the question mark?"

"Some of the photos go back a year. I thought this big day was in a few weeks."

Glad of a safe topic, Olivia explained. "The bicentennial celebration has been going on all year. The city sponsored a special event each month. It started with a poster contest—the winner is the one you see all over town. We held an arts and crafts festival, a citywide Thanksgiving dinner, and a huge Christmas celebration with lights all over the square. It's been all building up to the big day. Plus, there were smaller events organized by local businesses."

"Sounds like a lot of work. Were you involved in all of that?"

"In one way or another. It's been a wonderful experience."

"Better than teaching? I thought you loved that job."

Olivia faced him. "I was never a teacher.

I was an accountant for an insurance company."

Ben looked surprised. "I thought for sure you were…"

Olivia gritted her teeth. "That was Sunday school, and I only did that one time." The look of chagrin on his face gave her a moment of satisfaction. "Obviously there are many gaps in your memory."

"That's not true." He swung his chair around to look at her directly. "What I remember most is that we were always having fun and enjoying discovering things together."

She remembered only too well. Life with Ben had been a thrill a minute, fun and new discoveries around each corner. She'd never known anyone like him. He could turn anything into a party or an adventure. She had loved every moment with Ben, looked forward to a long life of laughter and happiness. Obviously, those were very unrealistic expectations.

"That was a long time ago, Ben. We're different people now."

He came toward her desk then lowered himself into a chair. "I've been wanting to ask you what you've been doing since…the last time I saw you."

Olivia nearly told him to mind his own business, but then decided it was time he knew what his rejection had brought about. "I grew up. I found a new career and new purpose." She hoped her tone had conveyed the idea that she had a new life and a better future since he walked out. "What about you, Ben?"

He sighed. "I traveled for a while and… I grew up. I had no choice."

Something in his voice sent a chill through her nerves. He'd said it as if the process had been difficult. Had the playboy been forced to give up his fun-loving ways? The shadows in his eyes were concerning. "Why did you really take this job? It can't be because you need the money." She sensed him stiffen.

"As a matter of fact, I do. I'm making my own way these days."

"Problems with your family?"

He inhaled slowly. "It's time for me to chart my own path."

He turned and looked at her, and she was caught in the dark expression in his eyes. She was seeing a different Ben. One she hadn't known before. A serious, sad and mature version. A man who may have known a crisis or suffered trauma. It didn't fit with the Ben she remembered. Maybe he was simply looking for sympathy. "Apparently, you've forgotten how to laugh."

He stood and slipped his hands into his pockets. "I laugh for different reasons now."

He turned and walked out of the office, leaving Olivia to wonder what he'd meant.

What had taken the joy out of the man she'd once known?

The moment Olivia stepped inside her bungalow that evening her tension melted away. All she wanted to do was have supper, then kick back and finish the suspense novel she was reading. She needed the escape more than ever today. After fixing a glass of sweet tea, she went to her front porch and settled onto the swing.

Her gaze wandered around her charming neighborhood and the pots on her steps with the bright yellow petunias she'd planted last week. April was the prettiest month of the year in Blessing. Every corner of every yard was bursting with color. The row of pale pink azaleas along her neighbor's driveway made her smile. Nora Lawrence had a green thumb.

As she set the swing in motion, an SUV pulled up in front of Nora's house. Olivia leaned forward. Was that? No. It couldn't be. Why would he be there? The vehicle stopped and a man got out. A tall man with broad shoulders and brown hair and a swagger when he walked.

Ben!

As if hearing her he turned and met her gaze across the tree-lined street. He didn't move. Didn't smile. Just stared at her with a sad expression.

Stunned, she hurried back inside, searching for an explanation. Did he know Nora? She'd only met the woman a couple of times since she'd moved in. As far as she knew, she had nothing to do with the birthday celebration.

There had to be an explanation, but for the life of her she couldn't come up with one that made any sense. A knock at her front door made her jump. She went toward it and saw Ben on the other side of the glass panels. Her stomach flipped over.

"May I come in? I think we need to talk."

Olivia raised her chin. "I'm tired. Maybe tomorrow."

Ben stood his ground. The only indication of his emotions was the subtle way he rubbed his thumb and fingers together. Odd that she should remember that.

"Please."

She stepped back and motioned him in.

He glanced around. "This is nice. It looks like you."

Olivia set her jaw. "And how would you know that?"

Ben bowed his head a moment then nodded. "Touché." He strode to the sofa and sat down, but remained on the edge leaning forward as if he wasn't going to stay long, much to her relief.

She sat in the armchair, creating space between them. She remembered the way his nearness always set her senses into turmoil. "What are you doing at Mrs. Lawrence's house?"

"That's one of the things I wanted to talk about. I'm staying there. She's my aunt."

Olivia frowned. "Your aunt? You never told me you had relatives in Blessing."

Ben raised his eyebrows. "Actually, I did. I mentioned that she was glad we were…that the ceremony was here, so she didn't have to travel."

Olivia shook her head. "No. You never told me that. I would have remembered."

"But you didn't."

Olivia wasn't in the mood to bicker. "Why are you here, Ben? What are you trying to accomplish? If you're hoping for a way back into my good graces you can forget it."

Ben wrung his hands. "Several reasons. I've never felt right about walking out. I thought it was best at the time, but I realized it was the worst thing I could have done."

"Yes, it was. So, are we done? You've apologized. You can go now." She started to stand but he waved her down.

"No. I need to explain and to try and make peace somehow."

"No need. I'm fine. However, if you're seeking forgiveness, I'm fresh out."

Olivia knew she shouldn't be so harsh and vindictive, but she found it hard to stop. Part of her wanted to hurt him the way he'd hurt her, even though she knew it wasn't the Christian thing to do.

"No, I don't expect that. I wanted to see if you were all right, to see if you were happy."

"Extremely."

Ben swiped his hand over his jaw. "You're not going to make this easy, are you?"

"Should I?"

"No." He stood and walked to the fireplace, resting his hand on the mantel. "Do you know the names of my brothers?"

"What does that have to do with anything?" He looked at her with a challenging expression. "Uh." She dug through her brain. "Kyle, John and one other."

"Kyle, Jeff and Nate."

"Oh. I remember only one of them was coming to the...church."

Ben faced her. "It's occurred to me in these last few days that there are gaps in our knowledge of each other. I thought you were a teacher."

She hated to admit it, but he had a point. She'd dismissed the notion as a result of the passage of time. But then again, "I didn't know you suffered from migraines."

Ben looked away. "Last night my aunt was talking about my uncle Ted, who passed away five years ago. She told me of things he liked and didn't, of his favorite foods and hobbies. She remembered the tiniest details about him." He held her gaze. "Do you know where I went to college, Olivia?"

Caught off guard, Olivia struggled to recall. "Alabama."

He grinned and his eyes sparkled. "Louisiana State. Geaux Tigers."

Olivia pursed her lips together. "What's your point?"

He sat on the sofa again, holding her gaze. "That *is* the point. We don't know anything about each other. I thought you were a teacher. I don't know your favorite color or food or if you have any hobbies. What do you know about me?"

Heat flooded her cheeks as she realized with a jolt that she knew very little. "You liked to have fun."

Ben scoffed. "That's like saying I'm a man."

"This is ridiculous."

"Olivia, maybe not getting married was the best thing that happened. Shouldn't people who want to spend their lives together know intimate things like hobbies, fears, insecurities, hopes and dreams?"

The realization was disturbing. Her chest squeezed as she began to comprehend what he was saying. He was right. "We never talked about serious things. Like, if you wanted a family or not." She hadn't meant to say that out loud, but it had been a question in the back of her mind from the moment they'd gotten engaged.

Ben clasped his hands together. "Yes. Like that. Don't you see—we had a whirlwind romance, caught up in the joy of being together, and we never looked beyond the moment. You can't build a future on having fun. I knew you'd hate me eventually and I didn't think I could endure that."

"And walking away was easier?"

"No. Not easy at all. But I think we were

too busy being in love to discuss anything important. I woke up each day eager to find the next thing that would make you laugh, that would surprise you and bring out your joy. You were fascinating."

"Until I wasn't."

"That's not why I left. I didn't wake up one day and not love you anymore."

Olivia grabbed a throw pillow and held it against her chest. "You woke up and discovered you were afraid of commitment."

"That was a part of it, but not in the way you think. I didn't want to be like my father. He's been married five times. I was afraid I might be like him."

Olivia stared at Ben. "I didn't know that."

"I left because I loved you. What if I woke up in a year and started looking for wife number two? I couldn't do that to you. All I wanted was to make you happy. I didn't think I could do that with my background."

Tears stung her eyes. "You left me."

"I know. But after I saw you that day, I couldn't go through with it."

Olivia met his gaze and saw only sincerity in his expression. "You were there? At the church?"

He nodded; his blue eyes were dark with regret. "Yes. I was dressed and ready. I was going to talk to you, then I remembered it was bad luck to see you before the ceremony. But I saw you across the hall. The door was open and you looked like a beautiful dream. You were so happy, you glowed. I knew I was incapable of keeping that look of joy on your face."

"You don't know that."

"Perhaps, but I didn't have an example to follow on being a good husband and father."

That was something Olivia understood. She had a poor role model of motherhood in her life. But she wasn't going to let Ben off that easily. "Nice speech, Ben. But I'm not buying it. You were always quick with the persuasive words."

The muscle in Ben's jaw flexed. "I have a suggestion if you'll listen to it."

She shrugged. Her nerves were worn thin. She had to get him out of her house.

"I'd like us to start over. As friends. We're going to be together for the next few weeks. Until then let's get to know one another as people."

It was a sensible idea and she hated that he'd come up with it. The Ben who had arrived in Blessing a short while ago was playing havoc with the one she held in her heart, and she wasn't sure yet what to do with that discovery.

When she didn't respond, Ben rose and went to the door. "Think about what I said, please."

She stood and joined him. "I can't promise anything."

He met her gaze and she saw a familiar glint in his blue eyes, that look of affection that had always made her feel warm and tingly all over and filled her with happiness. He raised his hand and pointed a finger. She inhaled sharply. She knew what was coming. He'd always touched her cheek with his finger then trailed it down the side of her face to her neck before kissing her good-night. She told herself to move. To step away. She prayed he wouldn't touch her because despite the emotional shell she'd maintained since he'd arrived, she knew she'd never be able to withstand his touch.

He lowered his hand. "I'll see you tomorrow."

Olivia closed the door behind him, then sagged against it as the tears flowed and she grieved for the love she'd lost.

Chapter Three

Aunt Nora was waiting for him at the kitchen table when he returned from Olivia's house. He knew she'd want a detailed report, but he wasn't sure he was up to it. He was still trying to decide if he'd made any difference or not.

"How did it go? I don't see any red marks or bruises on you."

"No, it didn't come to blows. But I'm not sure if I made any headway or not."

"Can you blame her?"

Ben shook his head. "No. I'm beginning to understand what I did and I'm not proud of the decision I made."

"Don't be too hard on yourself. You're not the first man to rush into marriage only to regret it later. At least you had sense enough to take a step back."

"And trample Olivia's heart in the process."

"And your own I suspect."

Ben couldn't deny that fact. He'd been shocked to realize that he'd never stopped loving Olivia. "She was the only thing keeping me sane when Davey and I were caught."

"Have you told her about that part of your life?"

Ben frowned and shook his head. "No. Don't plan on ever telling her."

"And what about your future plans? Will you tell her about that?"

"I don't know. Right now, I just want to calm the waters and try and find a way to work together."

Nora stood and carried her cup to the sink. "Just keep in mind, kiddo, that repairing trust takes a long time and more hard work than you think."

Once again, his aunt had proved right. He'd always considered himself a savvy guy when it came to handling women. But he was realizing that Olivia's hurt went deeper than he understood, and was beginning to wonder if he'd ever get past it.

Stretched out in bed later, he tried to sleep, but today's events had stirred up old boogeymen and he couldn't chase them away. He'd been blindsided by seeing the chained door and he'd been unable to ward off the memory. Thankfully, it didn't last long, but long enough to create concern and questions in Olivia's mind. He'd said the first thing that had come into his head, a fabrication that he'd now have to perpetuate while he was here.

Thankfully, Olivia hadn't pressed him. He didn't want her sucked up in that mess. Rolling onto his side, he began a prayer for strength and guidance, but even as he lifted up his petition, his mind began to sink into the dark place he tried so hard to avoid. If his mood hadn't improved by morning, he'd have to resort to medications. Maybe it was time to find a support group.

Sitting on the side of the bed, he unwrapped a peppermint candy and chomped down on it. He was supposed to let the hard candy melt slowly, but sometimes, he needed the sharp tang to jolt his mind into place.

A wave of guilt rose into his chest and lodged in his throat. Why hadn't he seen what his leaving would do to Olivia? To him, the wedding had been a big party, just like any other he'd attended back then. To her, it had been the culmination of a lifelong dream.

Another image surfaced in his mind, the slender shape of a friend and travel companion. A man who had suffered along with him, endured the darkness and the pain. A man who had brought him to his faith. A man he'd failed to save.

Ben woke with a shout, sitting up in bed, drenched in sweat, heart racing in his chest compressed with the weight of an anvil. He scraped his fingers across his scalp. He hadn't had that nightmare in months. Being around Olivia had dug up more than his feelings for her; it had dredged up all his guilt.

"Benton. Are you all right?"

The tapping on his bedroom door increased his heart rate. He'd awakened his aunt. Another misstep. It took him a moment to find his voice. "Yeah. I'm fine. Just a bad dream. Sorry to wake you." He waited to hear her leave, but she didn't.

"Ben, honey, maybe we should talk. Tomorrow."

"Sure. Go back to bed. Sorry."

He held his breath until he was sure she had walked away, then fell back on the mattress. He doubted he'd get any more sleep tonight. He closed his eyes, setting his mind to think about the event pictures he had to take, but all that came to mind was Olivia. She was dressed in a white gown with a long train and a cloudlike veil. He called her name, and when she turned around, he saw the anguish on her face, the tears streaming down her cheeks.

He rolled onto his back and stared at the ceiling. Time to start counting flowers on the wall.

Olivia sat at her desk the next morning rubbing her temple, hoping to ease the throbbing in her head. Thanks to Ben's visit last night she'd hardly slept a wink. Her mind kept replaying the things he'd said and his suggestion about their relationship. If only he would go away. Or better yet that he'd never come to Blessing in the first place.

"Good morning."

Olivia moaned as Marcy Jo breezed into her office. The woman's habitual cheerfulness wasn't welcome today.

"Uh-oh. Bad night huh?" She sat down across from the desk. "Care to share?"

"Not really." She looked at her friend, and the compassion in her dark eyes changed her mind. Maybe sharing with someone would help her sort things out. "Ben came to my house last night."

"Really? That's odd. What did he want?"

Olivia held up a hand and waved it. "No. Let me correct that. Ben walked across the street and came to my house."

Marcy Jo frowned. "What do you mean? He was lying in wait for you?"

"In a way. I saw him come home, and he pulled to a stop in front of the house across the street. Turns out, it's his aunt's and he's staying there while he's in Blessing."

"You mean he has family here in town? Did you know that? I mean, didn't he mention it when you made all the wedding plans?"

Olivia's self-esteem took a tumble. "He said he told me, but I don't remember that. How could I have missed it? Now, whenever I look out my window I'll see him over there."

Marcy Jo huffed. "So don't look out the window."

Olivia gave her a scowl. "Not helpful."

"Sorry. So, what did he want to talk about? Not work I'm guessing."

Olivia searched for a place to start. "He asked me if I knew where he went to college."

"Weird."

She bit her lip. "I didn't know. I didn't know his aunt lived across the street—I didn't know his favorite food or color or NFL team." She rubbed her forehead. "And he didn't know much about me either."

"How is that possible? You two were inseparable in those months. Though." She shrugged. "I often wondered if you were really in love or just caught up in the fun and romance of it all. I remember asking you questions about Ben, like did he want kids, or was he a believer, and you always said it wasn't important."

The truth of her friend's words twisted her heart. "At the time, I didn't think it was. Last night we discovered that we didn't know anything important about each other. Not the things you need to build a life together."

"Then maybe it's a good thing the wedding never happened."

Olivia stared out the window. That was probably true but there could have been a better way to end the relationship. She tucked her hair behind her ears and looked at Marcy Jo. "Ben suggested that we start over and take these weeks together to get to know each other then decide how to proceed after that."

"That sounds like a great idea. Very mature, actually."

"No, it doesn't. I can't trust him. I can't let my heart get ripped apart again."

"I understand but think about it. What's the worst that could happen? Either you'll learn that he wasn't the man you thought he was, and you part ways, or you learn he's really a great guy and you two decide to continue as friends."

It made an odd kind of sense. Get to know him, then decide. All she had to do was keep her heart guarded at all costs. The big question was, did she want to get to know him?

"He runs."

"What?"

Olivia tapped her pen on the desk. "I saw him first thing this morning. He came out on the porch and stared up at the sky a long time then stretched then started his run down the street. He used to scoff at runners."

"Good. That's the first new thing you've learned. You should start a list. Each time you learn something about Ben, write it down. A good list and a bad list. Then, when the bicentennial is over you can look at the list and decide what you want to do."

A list. That appealed to her sense of organization, and it felt proactive. "That's a good idea." She opened a new file on her computer, titled it *Ben List* and formed two columns. One labeled *Good* and one *Bad*. It would keep her on sound footing. It would be easy to see which column was the longest and help her decide.

"Thanks, Marcy Jo. I feel much better about Ben's idea."

"Good." She stood. "Glad I could help.

Keep me posted. I'm curious about which list will be longer."

Olivia already knew. The Bad list.

Ben was late getting to the office the next morning. His run usually cleared his head and warded off the depression that sometimes dogged his mind. Today he'd finished without the uplift in mood.

He was still concerned about whether Olivia would accept his suggestion to get to know each other. He believed that if they did, they could find a path back to some kind of relationship. He wasn't fool enough to think they could find a future together, but he'd settle for friendship.

He heard a familiar shrill voice as he approached Olivia's office.

"You are staying on top of this project, aren't you? It could mean the difference between you getting the job or not. You don't want to let this opportunity get away from you."

"Yes, mother. I know."

"I know you're meant for better things than this silly birthday committee. Why you wanted to work here is beyond me. But you've done well, and it's given you a shot at a more prestigious position. Once you're town manager then the sky is the limit. Do a good job and you could run for mayor."

"Mom, I don't want to be mayor of Blessing."

"Of course you do. Think of the power and prestige."

"Mother, please."

The pleading tone in Olivia's voice gave Ben the cue he needed to step forward. "Good morning. Where are we going today?"

The woman turned and stared at him, and Olivia gave him a grateful smile. "Good morning, Ben. You know my mother, Mrs. Marshall."

Ben nodded but before he could speak Olivia's mother glared at him. "You! What are you doing here? You have no business coming around my daughter after what you did."

"Mom, it's all right. Ben is working with me on a special project. Everything is fine."

"It's certainly not fine. He could ruin everything. He could undermine all your hard work. How do you know he's not here to destroy your future again?"

Ben winced and saw Olivia's eyes grow moist. "I assure you, Mrs. Marshall, I'm only here to help."

"I doubt that. I'm going to speak to your boss."

"Mom, no. Please don't. It's really fine."

Ben watched her mother storm from the office sending a scathing glance at him as she passed. "Should I go after her?"

Olivia sat down and tucked her hair behind her ears. "No. Delores will handle it. This has happened before."

Ben sat down, keeping an eye on Olivia. "Your mother is a forceful person."

Olivia fisted her hands on the desktop. "She's pushy and controlling and she thinks she's helping me get ahead."

"You don't want to be mayor of Blessing?"

"Hardly."

"What do you want?"

He saw her pull back. "Right now, I want to finish this booklet."

"I'm ready. Where do we go today?"

"The Blessing Bridge Prayer Garden. We need photos of the park with all the spring flowers in bloom. It's spectacular."

"Lead the way." They gathered up their equipment and headed for the parking lot. He could see she was still upset by her mother's visit. "Would you like me to drive today?"

She nodded.

Before he started the engine, he took a deep breath and braved the question that had kept him up all night. "Have you thought any more about my suggestion?" It took her a moment to respond. He held his breath.

"I think we should give it a try. We've got nothing to lose, right?"

Relief brought a smile to his face. "No. Nothing at all." Except the only woman he had truly loved. Maybe a trip to the prayer garden was exactly what he needed right now.

Olivia added two new facts about Ben to her list that evening as she ate supper. Into the Good column she wrote *kind*, *thoughtful*, then added *religious*, with a question mark.

She hadn't thanked him properly for the way he'd stepped in and eased her mother's tirade. She usually had to deal with her alone.

When they'd arrived at the Blessing Bridge, Ben had taken time to read the large plaque at the entrance that explained about the mother who had prayed at the bridge for healing for her son and seen him healed. Then people began to come to the bridge and lift up their petitions.

He'd asked questions and Olivia had told him how they'd almost lost the bridge when the land had been left to a distant relative of the original owner, but a change of heart had caused him to donate the land to the city.

Olivia had let Ben wander around, taking

his photos. She'd learned quickly to trust his skill behind the camera. What had surprised her was when he was done he'd spent a long time on the bridge in contemplation. It had seemed at odds with the man she'd known. Was that something else she'd missed seeing? Was Ben a man of faith?

She'd finally found the courage to ask him when they'd returned to the office. "I didn't realize you were a religious man."

He'd smiled. "Not religious. Just a sinner saved by grace."

She hadn't known how to respond. She knew what he meant but it was in conflict with her memory of him. Her own faith had taken a beating after being jilted. She'd railed at the Lord for putting Ben in her life if He wasn't going to let the marriage happen. She was only now, three years later, finding complete peace about the event. Though, Ben showing up had rattled her some. Still, she realized it wasn't the Lord who had prevented the wedding but her own failure to see through the romantic fog.

Olivia took a look at her lists and noted that nothing new had been added to the Bad column. She doubted it would stay empty long. No one was perfect. Especially not Ben Kincaid.

She had just drifted off to sleep when the loud banging on her front door started. Alarmed, she rose and hurried to the living room. Had something happened to Ben? Or Nora? Did he need help? There was no one else who would come to her house. Thankfully, her mother had left town and gone back to Birmingham.

She peeked out the window and saw her sister Loretta standing there.

"Sis. Open up."

Olivia stared at her older sister. "What are you doing here? How did you find me?"

Loretta pushed into the room. "Mom told me. I need your help. And I don't have much time."

"What's happened? Are you okay?" She looked her sister up and down, noting the flashy top and skin-hugging tights in bright yellow.

"Fine, but I need to leave Charlie here with you. I can't take him with me."

"Charlie?"

Loretta went back to the porch and brought a little boy into the house. He was clutching a red-and-blue plastic truck in his arms, and he looked terrified.

"My kid. He's four. I need you to take him."

She dropped a bag on the floor along with a suitcase.

"Take him?"

"Yeah. I'm getting married." She cocked her head. "I met this wonderful guy. He's handsome and rich, and he's going to take me to live on his estate in St. Thomas. But he only wants me. Not the kid."

Olivia struggled to find words. "I can't take him. I don't know anything about children."

"Not much to know. Please, Liv, I have a chance at happiness and I want to take it. You understand, don't you?"

"No. I don't. Why doesn't this man want your child?"

She waved off the comment. "He's not into kids. We have a life planned with travel and adventure and a kid just doesn't fit in."

"Why don't you leave him with mom?"

Loretta grimaced. "Are you kidding? She hates kids. She hated us."

Olivia couldn't disagree but that was a discussion for another time. "Loretta, I have a full-time job. I don't have time to watch a child." She glanced at the little boy. He was adorable, with his big blue eyes, button nose and shaggy blond hair. She knew her sister had been pregnant, but then she'd stopped communicating, and Olivia had heard nothing more for years.

"Then hire a nanny. You can afford it."

"What?"

Loretta looked around. "If you can afford this place you can afford a kid."

"No, I can't. I'm in the middle of a really busy time at work."

"You'll be fine. You were always the organized one. He's no trouble. He's quiet and doesn't talk much. I've got to go." She picked up her purse and turned to leave.

"Wait. What about his health? Is he allergic to anything? What does he eat? There are things I need to know."

"He's fine. Healthy as a horse. Thanks, sis." She walked out the door and Olivia darted after her. "Wait. You can't do this. Loretta, please."

It was only then, as her sister was getting into her car, that Olivia noticed Ben hurrying across the street. Loretta roared away from the curb and Ben jogged up on the porch.

"What's going on? Are you okay? Who was that?"

Olivia fought back panic and tears. Her mind struggled to adjust to what her sister had done. Ben lightly touched her arm. She looked at him and a wave of gratitude washed over her. She could use a good friend right now. Even if it was Ben.

"That was Loretta, my sister."

"You have a sister? Okay, what did she want?"

"She needed my help."

"With what?"

Olivia turned and walked inside, stopping in front of the chair Charlie was sitting in. "Him. He's my nephew, her son, Charlie. She's left him here with me. Permanently." The shock on his face mirrored her own. "Ben, what am I going to do? I don't know anything about small children."

"Why did she leave him?"

"She's getting married, and the man doesn't want the boy."

Ben rubbed his chin. "Can she do that? I mean, is it legal to just dump your child off with someone?"

Olivia chewed her thumbnail. "I'm his aunt so I suppose it's okay, but I've never been around little kids. I never even babysat. I don't know how to care for them and I can't stay home and watch him—I have too much work to do."

Ben put an arm around her shoulder. "Don't worry—we'll work it out."

He walked over to the chair and hunkered

down. "Hey, Charlie. I'm Ben. How old are you?" Charlie studied Ben a moment then slowly held up four fingers. Ben chuckled. "Wow. You are all grown up."

Charlie stared at him a moment. "You're big."

Ben chuckled. "I suppose I am. That's a nice truck you have there. It must be special."

Charlie nodded but didn't speak.

"Are you hungry?"

Charlie glanced at Olivia then nodded at Ben.

Ben stood and held out his hand. "Then let's go see what Aunt Olivia has in the kitchen."

He winked at her, and she followed him from the room. "I don't have anything a child would eat."

Ben helped Charlie into a chair at the table, then opened the fridge and pulled out a carton of milk. Charlie nodded. Taking the hint, Olivia took a few sugar-free cookies from the cupboard and put them on the table. Charlie stared at them a moment then started munching away like he hadn't eaten in a while.

Olivia drew Ben aside far enough so the boy didn't hear. "How did you know to do that?"

Ben shrugged. "He's a little boy. They're

always hungry." Ben's smile softened. "He's a cute one."

Olivia couldn't disagree. "He's so quiet."

"He's just been dumped with a stranger. Give him time. He'll warm to you."

She shook her head. "I don't know anything about being a mom, and what about all the work coming up with the bicentennial?"

Ben touched her chin with his fingertip. "Take a deep breath. It'll be all right. I'll be right here to help."

Even Ben's reassuring words couldn't stop the rising panic in her chest. "This isn't going to work."

"We'll make it work. For the little guy. He needs us, Livvy. He doesn't have anyone else."

"I don't know what to do."

"But I do. My brother Jeff has three kids. I stayed with him when I got back from…a while back. I'm no expert but I can handle the basics. Don't worry. We'll face this together. I won't let you deal with this alone. I'd better check on the little man."

Olivia watched him put more cookies on the plate, which earned him a small smile from her nephew. He was an adorable little guy. Her fears slowly ebbed as she watched the pair. Ben's assurance of help was profoundly reassuring.

She had one more item to add to her Good list.

Rescuer.

Chapter Four

The morning sunlight flooding into Olivia's bungalow living room usually lifted her spirits for the day, but her mind was too preoccupied to appreciate it. Her gaze kept going to the hall and her bedroom door where little Charlie was still sleeping. She and Ben had prepared a bed for him on the chaise in her spare room. Unfortunately, he didn't remain there all night. He woke her at midnight by standing beside her bed holding his truck and staring at her with big fearful eyes.

Her heart went out to him, and without thinking she lifted him into bed beside her where he'd snuggled close and fell sound asleep still clutching the truck. Poor little guy must have been exhausted because he was still sleeping. Taking another sip of her coffee she tried not to be overwhelmed by the thought of caring for Charlie full-time. She had a job, she was clueless and she was terrified of doing something wrong that might hurt her little nephew.

After a quick check to make sure he was all right, Olivia picked up her phone and called Delores. She had no idea how her boss would react or if she'd be willing to work around this new obligation. She was just winding up the call when Charlie dashed into the room and crawled up beside her on the sofa, scratching her arm slightly with his ever-present plastic truck.

"Ouch." She checked her skin but only found a slight red line. She looked at Charlie, who had that wide-eyed, fearful look in his blue eyes again. The thought shot through her mind that he might be afraid she would punish him. Harshly. Was that why he was so silent and withdrawn? Surely not. Her sister wouldn't harm her child or abuse him in any way. She put her arm around the boy and hugged him; the fear turned to a smile.

What had happened to this sweet little boy? Besides the fact that his mother dumped him with a stranger for who knows how long.

A wave of insecurity surged through her veins. Taking care of Charlie was one thing; dealing with a child who had emotional problems was something she wasn't equipped to handle.

After reaching for her phone, she called Ben. "I think Charlie may have been mistreated."

"Good morning to you too. What are you talking about?"

Olivia explained her impressions. "I don't know what to do for him. How do I handle this?"

"Sounds like you're doing just fine. You want me to come over?"

A sigh of relief escaped her lips before she realized it. "Yes. Please."

"I'll be there as soon as I can."

By the time Ben arrived, she and Charlie had eaten a breakfast of scrambled eggs, juice, toast and bacon. Charlie was hesitant at first, as if he'd never eaten eggs before, which made Olivia wonder what kind of care Loretta had been giving her son.

Ben stepped into the kitchen and went right to Charlie and smiled down at him. "Hey, buddy. Why didn't you tell me you were fixing breakfast? I would have come sooner."

Charlie smiled at Ben, then handed him the plastic truck sitting beside his plate. Ben exchanged looks with Olivia. It was the first time the child had let go of the toy. She smiled. Progress. Her chest warmed with a strange unfamiliar warmth. She liked the feeling.

Maybe caring for Charlie wouldn't be so bad after all.

"Can I fix you something, Ben?"

He shook his head. "Aunt Nora fed me up good." He sat down at the table and rolled the truck back and forth making engine sounds, which drew a giggle from Charlie.

"I talked to Delores this morning and explained the situation. She was more understanding than I expected considering our time frame for the celebration."

Ben nodded. "She called me after she spoke to you. There are a handful of static displays she wants me to photograph, so we can work independently today. We'll get together tomorrow and work out a schedule. Nora is free to watch our boy whenever we need her."

Our boy. The words left an odd bubble in her throat. She bit her lip.

Ben smiled at her. "You going to be okay today watching him? I can get back here quick if you need me, or you can get Nora if you need help. She said she'd be at the doctor's a short while this morning but after that she's free."

Olivia wasn't ready to admit it, but she was looking forward to watching her nephew today. Each time she looked at him her heart would go all mushy. It was very strange, but not unpleasant.

Her confidence grew during the morning. She'd gotten Charlie dressed and settled with his toys and had been working on her laptop for about half an hour when he came up to her and asked to go outside. Caught off guard, she tried to consider his request. Her backyard wasn't fenced, but she had a large front porch. "How about you play on the porch? You can take your truck and other toys out there."

Charlie smiled and nodded. "Is the big Ben man coming back?"

"Yes. He'll be here later. Did you like him?"

Charlie nodded and smiled.

Satisfied he was happy on the sisal rug on her porch, she went inside and moved her computer so she could see her nephew through the window. She was really getting the hang of this childcare thing.

The next time she looked up, she didn't see him. Assuming he was at the far end of the porch, she peeked out the front door windows. No Charlie. Alarmed, she went onto the porch. His toys were all there but no little boy. Terror exploded in her brain. "Charlie. Charlie!"

Darting down the front steps, she looked around the yard then jogged to the backyard to check there, but there was no sign of the child.

"Oh. No. Charlie! Where are you?"

Driven by fear she yelled louder, calling his name over and over. Nora's car was gone from the driveway so she couldn't turn to her for help. She went to the sidewalk and looked up and down the street. "Charlie!" Her stomach twisted. Had someone taken him? The thought buckled her knees.

When she looked down the street again, she saw an elderly man waving broadly at her, motioning for her to come toward him. Did he have her nephew? She broke into a run and exhaled in a loud rush when she saw Charlie sitting in the grass in the man's front yard. He was with a little girl and they were giggling and playing with a lively litter of puppies.

"I figured someone would be looking for the little guy."

Olivia tried to catch her breath and calm her racing heart. The man smiled. "He's fine. He saw my granddaughter Gracie pushing the pups in her doll carriage and followed her home. I hadn't seen him in the neighborhood so I figured he was a new arrival."

Finally able to breathe, Olivia nodded.

"He's my nephew. He's come to stay with me for a while."

The man introduced himself as Ron Sanders. "Well, he's welcome to come see the puppies whenever he wants."

"Thank you, but no. I'm keeping him inside from now on. I had no idea he could disappear so quickly."

Mr. Sanders chuckled. "It only takes the blink of an eye. Toddlers are quick little things."

Olivia let her gaze rest on Charlie and the wiggling dogs. He was giggling and hugging them. The sound of his laughter made her smile. He and Gracie rolled onto their stomachs and let the critters crawl over them, creating a fresh round of laughter. It was an adorable sight. But she had to get Charlie home. She couldn't relax until he was safe in the house.

It took a lot of persuading and reassurance from Mr. Sanders to convince the boy to go back to the house with Olivia. She promised to come again so he could play with Gracie and the pups.

Safely settled inside, Olivia tried to explain to Charlie why he shouldn't leave the house, but quickly realized it was difficult to reason with a four year old. Now that the incident was over, her mind was filled with thoughts of all the horrible things that could have happened if not for the kindness of her neighbor. She was in desperate need of reassurance. Without realizing what she was doing, she placed a call to Ben and shared her ordeal.

"Ben, he just wandered off. Why would he do that?"

"Because he's four. He's all right, isn't he?"

"Yes." Her gaze went to her nephew, who was playing with his truck on the carpet. She'd kept him in eyesight every second since bringing him home.

"How about you? Have you recovered from the scare?"

She closed her eyes and fought the rush of guilt that rose every time she thought about him wandering off. "I suppose. I knew I couldn't do this. I don't know anything about kids."

"Livvy, you did everything right. You found him and you brought him home and he's fine."

His calm, reassuring tone eased much of her concern. "I should never have left him on the porch. But I never dreamed…" She sighed.

"Don't be so hard on yourself. This has happened to every parent at one time or another."

"Are you sure?" She looked at Charlie, who had swapped the truck and had set up a line of small cars across the rug. He was happy and content as if nothing had happened. Ben's voice in her ear reclaimed her attention.

"I should have said something. I lost track of my nephew once in a hardware store. Worst experience of my life."

"What did you do?"

"Same as you. Started yelling for him and found him one aisle over looking at garden gnomes. I never let him out of my sight after that."

Olivia sighed. "When I think of what could have happened, I get sick to my stomach."

"No. Don't do that. It's all good. You'll just be more aware next time. I'll pick up a safety gate for the front porch, but you might want to think about fencing the backyard so he can play and not get away. I need to go. I still have to shoot the birthday wall and the committee chairman wants pictures."

"Thanks, Ben. I feel better. Oh, Charlie says hi, Big Ben. Apparently, that's his name for you."

Ben chuckled. "I like it. See you later."

The rest of the day was exhausting. Olivia kept her nephew in sight every moment. By the end of the day, she felt like she'd aged ten years. How did parents live like this? She was obviously not designed to be a parent.

And yet, she couldn't deny that her heart became oddly warm when she looked at him. She just didn't know if that was a good thing or not.

Ben changed the settings on his Canon, then aimed it at the side of the old brick building that ran the length of the block along Liberty Street. The expanse of wall had been chosen as the Birthday Wish Wall, a place for residents to leave comments about the coming bicentennial event.

Ben's ringtone sounded and he pulled the cell from his pocket expecting to see Olivia's name on the screen again. He'd wondered how she'd been getting along with Charlie after his adventure and had been tempted to call. Ultimately, he'd decided that checking in on her might make her feel as if he was doubting her ability to handle the situation. He wanted to build her up, not discourage her.

His mood shifted when he saw his brother's name on his phone screen. He hesitated a moment, draping his camera around his neck before answering the call. "Hey, Jeff."

"You sound awful. I guess things aren't going well with Olivia?"

Ben pulled up his emotional guard. Jeff was the only member of the family who understood what he'd been through and where he wanted to go, but he tended to be overly concerned, which could be irritating. "Slowly."

Jeff groaned softly. "I don't like that tone. Are you okay?"

"Of course. Why wouldn't I be?"

"I can think of three reasons off the top of my head. One, you left your treatment early. Two, you still need emotional support, and three, because you walked into another guilt-ridden situation that you might not be prepared for. How am I doing?"

Ben rubbed his forehead. His brother worried too much. "It's fine. Things here aren't as bad as I expected."

"Olivia has forgiven you already?"

"Hardly. But we've declared a truce for the time being."

"How's that going to help?"

"Not sure. I'm playing it by ear for the time being."

"I don't like it. This is too risky for you right now. You don't need any more guilt."

"Jeff, I'm good. Aunt Nora has been helpful, but yeah. I had no real idea what I had done to Olivia when I walked out. I don't think I could ever make it up to her."

"Of course not. You can't go back and fix it either. I'm not sure what you hope to accomplish by being there with her."

"Peace. That's all I ever wanted."

"All right, let's say you find it with Olivia. You can't turn back time and make peace with Davey."

Ben fought the sudden urge to hang up on his brother. Jeff had been a blessing during his therapy with his blunt and honest approach. But he didn't need that right now. "One thing at a time. That's all I can do."

"Ben, come home. Don't subject yourself to this pain."

"I appreciate your concern, but I've got things under control. I've found a church and a group. And I always have my peppermints."

Ben ended the call over his brother's protest, then sat on a park bench and stared at his camera. He'd lied. Each moment with Olivia was pricked with guilt. Thankfully, their truce and the arrival of Charlie had diverted much of that.

He found himself learning new things about her every day, like how confident and outgoing she'd become. And yet those qualities brought to mind how sweet and unsophisticated she'd been. He wasn't sure if that was a good thing or not. He'd forced her to become someone else. Then again, everyone grew and changed. He surely had. Deep down he believed Olivia was still the loving and caring woman he'd fallen for.

Now Charlie had been added to the equation. The little guy had captured his affection immediately. He understood what it was like to be suddenly left in a strange place and the fears that surrounded you in the dark when you were all alone. What the little boy needed now was to feel safe and cared for, and he and Olivia would make sure of that.

He thought back to when he'd stayed with Jeff. He'd come to enjoy his nephews. They'd given him a joy he'd never known and kept his mind from sliding into those dark places that were hard to dig out of.

He pulled a peppermint from his pocket and started to unwrap it. Charlie would be a nice diversion. And give him a reason to stay close to Olivia.

His time with her was short, and he wanted to make the most of every moment.

Olivia poured a small glass of milk and placed a banana beside it, watching as Charlie attacked his food. He always ate as if he was afraid he wouldn't get any more. Her concern for him was growing. She'd tried to call

Loretta, but the phone was no longer active. She needed to discuss this with Ben.

A knock on the door interrupted her worries. She was pleased and surprised to find Nora on her doorstep. She welcomed her in.

Nora gave her a quick hug. "I thought it was time I met our new visitor. Ben says he's a real little charmer."

Olivia smiled. "He is that. Come on in. He's having a snack."

Olivia watched as Nora made friends with her nephew. He took to the older woman right away, which eased Olivia's concerns about Nora watching him. They moved to the living room when Charlie finished his snack. He settled in to play, bringing his toys to Nora to show her. Once Charlie was out of hearing, Olivia took the opportunity to ask Nora's advice. She bit her bottom lip, trying to find a place to start. "Nora, does Charlie seem okay, I mean normal, to you?"

"How do you mean?"

"He seems so quiet and a bit skittish. I'm worried about the kind of care he'd been getting."

Nora nodded and looked at the child. "Do you think he's been neglected in some way?"

"Maybe. I don't want to think that my sister would mistreat her child, but his truck scratched me and he looked at me like he was afraid I'd hit him, and he gobbles his food like it might disappear."

"Does he talk to you much?" Nora handed Charlie the car he'd brought to her.

"Not really. He'll answer when I ask him something. But he doesn't initiate conversation. He asks about Ben often."

As if aware that he was being talked about, Charlie came and stood beside Olivia, leaning against her knee and holding a small car from his toy collection. Olivia slid her arm around him and he looked up at her with a smile.

Nora chuckled. "He seems comfortable with you. But if you're really concerned, make an appointment with a pediatrician and have him checked out. Dr. Knudson is the best."

"Maybe I should." It was a sensible suggestion, and it would go a long way to answering her questions about his health.

Olivia told Nora about Charlie's wandering off. Nora chuckled and patted Olivia's knee.

"Welcome to the club, dear. You've passed your first challenge. It doesn't mean you're doing a poor job—it just means you're caring for a toddler." Nora stood to go. "In the meantime, give him extra attention, play with him, read to him, maybe pick up some educational toys, like numbers and letters, animals. Maybe all he needs is attention and being made to feel safe and secure."

"That's what Ben said. It sounds so simple."

"It is." Nora smiled. "Isn't that what we all want deep down, to feel safe and secure and know that we're loved?"

Olivia took Nora's suggestion to heart and went online and searched for educational toys for four year olds. She had a cart full of items when Ben knocked on the door later.

Charlie looked up as Ben came through the door, then rushed to meet him, his little arms in the air to be picked up. Ben gathered him up and received a tight hug around his neck. "I'm glad to see you too, little buddy."

Olivia's heart grew warm and soft. The sight created emotions inside that she'd never fully considered. A family. It was something she'd avoided thinking of after the failed wedding.

Ben put Charlie down and came toward her with a smile and a hint of concern in his eyes.

"How are you doing? All over your scare with Charlie?"

It was like him to think of her. He'd always been so thoughtful—well, most of the time. She returned his smile. "I am. Nora came by and we talked. She gave me several suggestions to help Charlie feel more secure."

"Big Ben, come see my cars."

"Okay, buddy." Ben joined the little boy on the floor and examined each little car he was handed.

Olivia smiled. The domestic scene had spawned that warm fuzzy sensation in her chest again. It happened each time she saw them together, and when Charlie smiled, or giggled. To be honest, it happened every time she looked at him.

She turned, intending to join the two, but her gaze landed on the small calendar on her sofa table. The date sent a sudden chill down her spine. The big celebration was right around the corner. Which meant that once the bicentennial was over, Ben would be gone. He'd hired on for the event. Nothing more.

Her mind spiraled back in time. Ben would disappear from her life again, leaving behind a hole in her world. In just a short amount of time she'd forgotten the past and allowed Ben to worm his way into her emotions again.

Charlie giggled and a new realization slammed into her. How would her little nephew handle Ben walking out of his life?

She inhaled and rested her hand at her throat. How had she let this happen? She'd gotten caught up in his charm and his help with Charlie and now she was allowing him deeper into her life. It had to stop. She had to think of her heart and of Charlie's heart. Her first responsibility was to protect him from being hurt.

The best way to do that was to end her reliance on Ben for help. Tomorrow she'd look into day care for Charlie. It was too dangerous to start depending on Ben. It would only end in heartache again.

Her gaze landed on the pair sitting on the floor surrounded by toys. And it started here and now. These faux family moments had to end. She needed to regain control of the situation. Charlie had been left in her care, not Ben's.

"Charlie, it's time for supper. Go wash your hands." The boy left the room, as she faced Ben and gripped all her resolve when she looked at him. "I'd invite you to stay but I only have enough for the two of us."

The look of surprise mixed with disappointment was nearly her undoing. She had to look at the bigger picture. "Thank you for your help today. I think after Charlie's little adventure this morning I can handle anything else that comes up."

Ben studied her a moment. "I'm sure you

can." He glanced around awkwardly. "Uh, well, I guess I'll see you tomorrow. I think Delores wants us to cover the kickoff of the Rock On event at the courthouse. Hey, why don't we let Charlie participate? He might like that."

Olivia struggled to remain firm. Her emotions were like a taffy pull. Part of her wanted to be excited about his suggestion, but the other side just wanted him out of her house so she could let down her guard and breathe. "I'll think about it."

The Rock On event was the brainchild of the local fire chief. He'd suggested that residents bring rocks to the courthouse park, paint something on them such as a saying, a picture or a prayer and when the celebration was over they would create a rock garden where all the rocks would be displayed.

"Good. Hey, buddy, I'll see you tomorrow, okay?"

Charlie came in and ran over to Ben, hugging him for a long time, making Olivia feel as if she was being the meanest aunt ever. But a small sacrifice tonight could save the little boy's heart down the road.

Olivia opened the door. "Thanks again, Ben."

The frown on his face stung. He nodded

then turned and left. She shut the door behind him, feeling as if she'd just made a very big mistake.

Apparently, being a good parent meant doing the hard stuff along the way.

Gobsmacked. That was the only word to describe the way Ben felt. He went back over his visit with Olivia as he crossed the street. She'd welcomed him, she'd smiled, everything had been normal, then suddenly she'd turned stiff and cold and practically ordered him from the house. Try as he might, he couldn't find a reason for her abrupt change in mood.

Nora was sitting in the living room, watching an old movie when he walked in. His confusion must have been visible on his face because one glance at him and she muttered under her breath and turned off the TV. "What happened? Everyone all right?"

Ben sank into the recliner, resting his elbows on his knees. "She threw me out."

Nora frowned. "Why?"

He shrugged. "I have no idea. I've been over it, but I can't find anything that I said or did that caused it. She changed so fast. Like flipping a switch."

Nora nodded then gave him her full attention. "Tell me everything that happened. Don't leave anything out."

Ben gave her a blow-by-blow, hoping she'd have some insight because he not only felt totally rejected, but he was already missing his little buddy.

"What if she won't let me see Charlie anymore? I look forward to seeing that little guy every day."

Nora held up a finger. "Maybe that's it."

"What do you mean?"

"Before Charlie came, what was your main goal?"

"To make peace with Olivia. But we've made up. We're enjoying each other again."

Nora nodded. "Exactly, and how much longer are you going be here in Blessing? Three or four weeks at most."

"Yes. I'm due in Jackson not long afterward."

"Which means you'll be gone from Olivia's life again. And from Charlie's."

"Yes, but not gone forever. I plan on coming back often. I wouldn't just disappear."

Nora raised her eyebrows. "Like you did before? Ben, your track record with Olivia is bad and if you think a few work assignments and fun time with little Charlie can erase all that, you're sadly mistaken. If I had to guess, I'd say something happened while you were there that made her realize that she still couldn't trust you completely. She's looking out for Charlie as well. The little guy is bonding with the two of you. You'll be leaving before long. Then what'll happen to him? He won't understand why you suddenly left. She probably thought about you leaving and worried that Charlie would have his heart broken."

"So she kicked me out?"

Nora shrugged. "More like pushing you away to protect her and Charlie from being hurt."

Ben shook his head. "How long will she doubt me?"

"A lifetime."

Ben groaned then stood and paced the room.

"If you still love her, and I think you do, then you need to call on all the patience you have and ask the Good Lord for an extra portion."

"Basically, you're saying, there's no hope?"

"No, not at all. But you'll have to be consistent and probably prove to Olivia many times that you can be trusted."

Ben rubbed his palm against his fist. "We don't have as much time together as we did.

We're working different schedules. That doesn't make it easy to get to know each other like we planned."

"Maybe it's time to tell her about your future plans."

"No. Not yet."

"Why not?"

"Sharing my decision hasn't gone well in the past when I told friends and family. It was a dead-end street to several of those relationships."

"I know, but Olivia isn't like them. I'd venture to say she'd be supportive."

Ben shrugged. "She's not the woman I remember. She's stronger and more independent. She probably has a whole new perspective on things."

"Don't anticipate trouble, kiddo. Olivia is a compassionate and understanding woman. Or else she wouldn't be caring for her nephew." Nora stood. "Maybe telling her your plans will help bridge the gap between you."

"Maybe, but I need to explain some things first, make her understand, then we'll see." He gave his aunt a hug. "I think I'll go to family night supper at the church. They're having catfish."

Nora patted his hand. "Enjoy."

Ben stared out his bedroom window later

that night at the dark little bungalow across the street. He'd looked over there half a dozen times this evening, watching as the lights went on and off, imagining Olivia and Charlie going through their nightly routine before finally turning out the lights when it was time to sleep. He wanted to be a part of it. Every little moment. He'd never felt so much a part of things as he did when he was with Livvy and Charlie. It was a feeling he didn't want to lose. Somehow, he had to find a way to hang on to it—forever.

Nora was right; he was beginning to understand it would take more than his own willpower to make it happen. Knowing when to ask for help was one of the biggest lessons he'd learned during recovery from his ordeal.

Chapter Five

Olivia ran a brush through her hair, then slipped on her favorite sea-glass earrings that complemented her green top. She'd been on the phone all morning and found a local childcare facility that would take Charlie for the day. Her heart twisted with regret. She didn't want to subject her nephew to yet another unfamiliar experience, but she had to work and after last night, relying on Ben for help was too risky. He threatened both their hearts.

As she passed by the front door on her way to find Charlie, her gaze landed on Nora's house. She wished she could trust Ben because she really needed his help. He'd told her his aunt would love to watch Charlie while they worked but she was too close to Ben to risk that arrangement.

She squared her shoulders. She didn't need Ben. She could manage without him, but she wasn't sure how to deal with Charlie's affections. When she'd put him to bed last night, he'd begged for Ben to come and say goodnight, and he'd refused to accept any explanation for her not calling him. She realized at that point that she'd do anything for the little boy, even break her own rules to make him happy.

She finally caved and called but it went to voice mail. Assuming he'd turned it off to avoid her, she called Nora only to be told Ben was attending family night supper at his church.

The information surprised and puzzled her. She didn't remember Ben being a man of faith. Had he changed so completely? There was that moment on the bridge when he had lingered, but that could have been nothing more than him enjoying the scenery. She found it unlikely that Ben had suddenly experienced a road to Damascus conversion.

A short while later, Olivia walked back to her car, her heart filled with tiny holes. She'd just abandoned Charlie to a bunch of strangers at the day care. He'd been a little hesitant to stay but the woman in charge was truly kind and gentle. Olivia had managed to convince him to trade his ever-present large plastic truck for a small car he could keep in his pocket, which she'd told him to squeeze whenever he felt lonely.

By the time she pulled up at the office she had labeled herself the worst, most heartless aunt on the planet and had decided to tell Delores she couldn't work today. But when she stepped into her boss's office, Ben was waiting for her and Delores was on the phone.

Ben gave her a hesitant smile. "Morning."

She could barely speak for the large lump in her throat. "Hello."

"Where's Charlie?"

"Day care. They take children on a drop-in basis."

Ben's jaw flexed. "Like dropping off dry cleaning?"

Before she could think of a reply, he held up his hand and apologized. "Sorry. I…"

Delores hung up the phone and faced them. "Okay, I need you to get over to the library. Our local celebrity, that ballplayer DeLong Graham, has written a book about his life in the NFL and he's here and being interviewed by the *Blessing Banner* and then he'll be signing copies of his book. I'd like some pics to be in that souvenir booklet." She glanced up at them. "There's an invitation-only meet and greet tonight at the Lady Banks Inn. Get shots of that too."

Olivia frowned. "I wasn't planning on including him in the booklet. I wanted to focus on the birthday events. He's just a lure to get more visitors."

Delores stared at her over the rim of her glasses. "I know that. But he's also our most famous resident and including him will keep Blessing in people's minds." She waved her hand. "Just get a bunch of pictures and we'll decide what to do later."

"We're on it." Ben took her elbow and steered her out of the office. "So do we go together or alone?"

The tone of his voice told her he was teasing her about the first assignment they'd had. She would like nothing more than to work separately, but that would be unproductive. "The library is one block over."

Ben nodded. "Then I could walk two steps behind if that would help."

Olivia stifled the smile on her lips. She was trying to keep her distance again, for her sake and Charlie's, but there was something about Ben that kept dismantling her resolve. "That won't be necessary."

After retrieving her purse and satchel from

her office they started out. Ben was silent as they walked but she knew that wouldn't last.

"How's Charlie?"

"He's fine. I checked with the day care and he's okay."

"I miss seeing him."

The sadness in his tone touched her. She hadn't thought about Ben's side of things. He'd bonded with her nephew quickly. If she kept her barriers in place, it would hurt them both, but she had to think about the future. "He wanted you to tuck him in last night."

"Really? You should have called me."

"I did. Your phone was turned off and Nora said you were at church." He didn't answer right away as if gauging his words.

"Yeah. If I'd known, I'd have come right over but…"

Olivia stopped and faced him. "I know I was rude last night, but I realized that you'll be gone soon and I worried what would happen to Charlie when you suddenly disappear. I don't want him hurt."

"Neither do I. I won't just walk away."

"You did once."

Ben took her hand. "And I was wrong. I promise I won't do that again, not to you or to Charlie."

A rush of memories coursed up her nerves

as he held her hand. All of them sweet and beautiful until they reached her heart where they turned scorched and bitter. She pulled her hand away.

"Don't deny me time with Charlie. Please, Livvy."

She didn't bother to correct him about her name. For some reason it didn't bother her like it had the first time. She started to walk again, trying to weigh her options. She had to protect Charlie but he loved Ben. Maybe there was a way she could prepare him for Ben leaving. Yet she couldn't deny that from a selfish standpoint she really could use his help. She might feel more confident about taking care of her nephew, because she still had a lot to learn.

"Let's take it one day at a time for now."

"Deal."

Olivia had counted on the author event keeping her busy but instead it only left her feeling confused and frustrated. They arrived at the library to find a half dozen journalists already there clamoring for interviews. Several from as far away as Jackson and Tupelo. She was ready to turn and leave but Ben waded in with enthusiasm and somehow found a way to get in front of the other photographers.

She stared in puzzlement at the scene. Who would have thought that a football player would cause such a frenzy in a small town? Accepting the inevitable, Olivia left Ben to do his thing and she took a seat in the corner.

Ben's plea to not cut him off from Charlie replayed in her mind. If the situation was reversed, she'd be asking for the same consideration. Could she in good conscience keep them apart? She'd weighed the pros and cons over and over by the time Ben rejoined her.

"I think I got some good shots of Mr. Quarterback. Delores should be pleased."

"Who?"

"Graham. The author."

"Oh, right. Delores wants us back at the office." Things between her and Ben were still strained, and she knew she couldn't let it stay this way.

Ben dangled his camera around his neck. "Lead the way."

They started down the sidewalk and Olivia could sense Ben's sideways glances in her direction. She might as well get this over with. "I've been thinking."

"Thinking is good. Sometimes."

He smiled and those dimples popped out. She really needed to strengthen her defenses where he was concerned. "I don't want to keep you from seeing Charlie, but we have to agree to prepare him for your leaving. I can't allow his little heart to be broken."

"I understand. I don't want to hurt that little guy. Thank you."

They stopped at the intersection to wait for the light. The rumble of a large truck drew near. Ben turned to look and froze. The truck lumbered by; its engine coughed and sputtered loudly as it passed, leaving a heavy cloud of diesel exhaust in its wake.

The light changed and Olivia stepped off the curb only to realize Ben hadn't moved. He stood still, staring at the ground; his hands were tightly fisted and he was breathing rapidly.

She went to him. "Ben. What is it?" Slowly his head lifted; he looked at her then nodded. His gaze clearing.

"Yeah. I'm good. Just lost in thought for a second."

It was a lie but she wasn't about to press him for an explanation here on the street corner. He glanced at the light. "We'd better go." He stepped off the curb and started across the street, slipping his hand into his pocket and pulling out a peppermint candy.

Olivia watched him unwrap it with shaky hands and put it in his mouth. "I've been meaning to ask you about your addiction to that sweet. When did you get so fond of peppermint?"

When he didn't answer she glanced at him. "Ben?"

He shrugged. "Overseas. They had a really good kind of peppermint there."

It was clear from his tone that he wasn't telling her everything. She had a bad feeling that whatever was going on wasn't good. For the first time since he'd returned, she began to wonder if he was all right.

From time to time she'd caught a glimpse of deep pain in his eyes that didn't used to be there. What had happened to him during those three years they were apart?

She dismissed her curiosity and reminded herself that she needed to concentrate on her work and not Ben Kincaid.

After all, she didn't need to know everything about him.

The rest of the week passed quickly, and thanks to Nora, Charlie didn't have to go back to the day care. He stayed with Nora and was happy as a lark. He looked forward to going to her house every morning.

Olivia glanced down at her nephew, who was playing with his beloved truck on the living room floor. Today, however, was Saturday and she planned to relax and take advantage of the lull and get caught up on work and rest. She never knew when Delores would call with something needing done.

Booting up her laptop, she then clicked on her Ben file and opened it, scrolling through the words she'd collected. The Good and Bad columns were nearly equal. To be fair, the Bad list had been written right after she'd started the file and contained words like *untrustworthy, selfish, can't commit, shallow, hard-hearted, cruel, mean* and *arrogant*. Those were all her old opinions, the ones she'd formed after the failed wedding. Were they true of the man today?

Only one of those words applied today. Untrustworthy. But that was the main issue.

She'd learned more about him this week, little odds and ends, like that he loved peppermint candy. He kept them in his pocket at all times. She'd added *likes kids, professional* and *dedicated* to the list of good things.

Off the list she'd learned he hated lasagna, loved blueberry ice cream and sour pickles. She'd learned he'd gotten his private pilot's license, he liked to cook and he was a fan of the New Orleans Saints football team. Sadly, none of the things in the Good column meant much without the one quality that mattered. Trust.

What troubled her now was his odd behavior in town. He'd zoned out again with no reasonable explanation. Even his comment about loving the little round peppermints seemed off.

As long as she had questions about Ben, she'd keep her guard up. Her heart couldn't handle any more unexpected issues where he was concerned. There was still tension between her and Ben; she knew it was her fault. She was keeping her shield firmly in place, but that got harder every day.

She closed her laptop and looked down at her nephew, who was now playing with the puzzles she'd bought him. He'd taken to all the educational toys she'd purchased and he was talking up a storm now. Nora said his vocabulary expanded daily. Her nephew was a smart little fellow. A swell of pride ballooned in her chest, though she could take no credit for that. The Lord had blessed the little boy with a happy spirit and a curious mind.

Charlie jumped up when a knock came on the door. Olivia opened it to a smiling Ben holding a black-and-white dog. Charlie pushed past her and looked up at Ben, reaching for the dog.

"Puppy."

Ben held the animal against his chest, gently scratching his head. "This is Rudy, and he needs a friend."

Charlie's smile grew. "I'll be his friend."

Ben put the dog on the floor and Charlie laughed when Rudy sniffed his chin.

Olivia couldn't help but smile at her nephew but she turned a stern eye toward Ben. "I can't take care of a dog. Why would you do this without talking to me first?"

Ben favored her with a sheepish expression. "I know, but it came up suddenly and Aunt Nora told me a pet might give Charlie a sense of security."

She crossed her arms over her chest. "I suppose, but I know less about pets than children. And I don't want the hassle or the mess."

"No problem. The dog is housebroken and he's great with kids and been through obedience school." Ben flashed a smile. "Look at it this way, if he has his own puppy he won't wander off to see the ones up the street."

Oh, those dimples. It was all she could do to maintain a serious expression.

He touched her arm lightly. "I knew you'd have reservations but give it twenty-four hours and see how it goes. If you still feel you don't want the dog, Aunt Nora said he can live with us and Charlie can play with him whenever he wants. He's at her house a good bit now anyway."

It was a sensible solution, and looking at the big smile on Charlie's face she wasn't sure she could take the animal away from him. A new thought surfaced. "I don't have food or bowls or a bed or leash, none of that."

Ben grinned, flashing those dimples that were always her undoing. "I've got it."

"Of course you do."

"I'll bring it in." He looked at Charlie then leaned toward her. "They look like best friends already."

She pursed her lips together and glared. But he'd already turned and walked out. She shouted over her shoulder. "He'd better not bark all night."

Her gaze landed on Charlie again and she had to smile. He was on his knees in front of the dog showing him all his special toys. Rudy was sitting patiently as if he was truly interested.

"I think I've just become a pet owner."

No matter what she tried, or what she vowed to do, Ben would somehow disrupt her life.

She had to find her inner strength again. Dimples or no dimples.

* * *

Ben jogged up the steps to Nora's and stopped on the porch when he felt his phone vibrate. He groaned when he saw his father's name on the screen and considered ignoring it, but that usually only made things worse. "Hey, Dad."

"Are you still in that backwoods town?"

"Yes. What do you want?"

"I have an offer you can't refuse. My casino host just quit and you'd be perfect for the job. I'll pay you twice what I paid him. How soon can you come home?"

Ben sighed and sat down on the swing, too tired to face this conversation. "No thanks, Dad. I'm good where I am."

His father grunted loudly. "No, you're not. It's time you gave up this nonsense you've adopted and get yourself back to a normal life."

"I like my life." He winced when his father cut loose with a string of expletives.

"I didn't raise you to be a wimp who needs a crutch to get him through the day. You survived and I thought you'd come back a man not a weakling. When are you going to wake up and see it's all a big scam?"

"That's your opinion."

"Are you getting back together with that mousy woman you were going to marry?

She's all wrong for you. I need you back here where you can meet a woman with class."

"Dad, you don't understand."

"I understand one thing. If you don't come back, I'm done with you. Don't come looking for help from me because you won't get it. Do you understand? I'm done."

The call ended and Ben inhaled a deep breath to calm his nerves. The screen door creaked and he looked up to see his aunt peeking out. "You heard, huh?"

"Hard not to." She joined him on the swing and patted his knee. "I wish I could explain my brother to you but I can't. He's always been a self-centered person with little regard for others. We weren't raised that way. I have no explanation."

"None needed. I knew what I was facing with the family when I told them my future plans."

Nora smiled and nudged him with her shoulder. "I'm so proud of you. I won't write you off. It's a real man to face what you are. Love you, kiddo." She stood and went back inside and Ben offered up thankful prayer. At least one member of the family stood by him. His gaze drifted across the street. Time to steel himself for being near Olivia.

How would she react when she learned of

the vocation he'd chosen? Would she be on the walk-away side like his former girlfriend or the stand-and-support side like Nora?

He'd probably never know because he didn't plan on telling her. His goal here was to make peace. The future had no place between them.

Olivia stepped out onto her front porch the next morning and saw Ben talking to his aunt. Charlie saw him too.

"Hey, Big Ben." He waved frantically.

Ben turned and smiled. Even from this distance she could see the dimples. He waved then came across the street.

"Good morning. Are you headed to church?"

Charlie nodded. "They have good stories about superheroes there."

Ben nodded. "I know."

Charlie took Ben's hand. "Come with me."

Olivia quickly tempered the invitation. "Oh, that's okay. Ben may have things to do this morning."

Ben stooped down and spoke to the boy. "That's the nicest invitation I've ever had." He glanced up at her. "I'd love to come with you."

Charlie grinned. "We're gonna walk."

Olivia wished she hadn't made such a big deal out of the warm weather this morning. "It's such a nice day and the church isn't that far."

"I agree." He fell into step beside Olivia as Charlie skipped ahead, humming a tune.

Olivia debated whether to ask a personal question then remembered that they were supposed to be learning about one another. "I haven't seen you at church before."

"No. You attend Blessing Community, I go to Oak Grove Church."

It was a much smaller congregation on the opposite side of town. "I know Pastor Shields. He's very active in the town. Marcy Jo goes there."

Ben nodded. "I've seen her."

Olivia bit her lip. "If you'd rather go there, I certainly understand."

He gave her a sardonic grin. "Trying to get rid of me?"

She bristled. "Of course not. But I know how important it is to feel at home in a church."

"True, but it's also nice to visit other congregations. I'm told Pastor Miller delivers a great sermon."

"He does."

They crossed the street and entered the old

brick church from the side entrance closest to Charlie's toddler Sunday School Class. He ran into the room, barely saying goodbye.

Ben chuckled. "I guess he likes his class."

She nodded. "He loves being with other children. I think he's going to be a very social young man."

"That's a big change from the day he arrived. He's happy with you, Olivia."

The compliment warmed her heart. "I hope so."

They entered the sanctuary near the front and Ben took a seat in the second row, which surprised her. She usually tried to find a seat in the middle or toward the back. She settled in beside him just as the praise band started to play.

The service progressed and Pastor Miller reminded the congregation that they would be continuing their study of Romans. Ben pulled his cell phone from his pocket and started swiping. She was about to remind him that he was at church when she glanced at the screen and realized he had pulled up an online Bible.

He listened intently as the pastor spoke, checking his cell screen and following along with every reading of a passage. She rarely did that. She did better when she concentrated on the spoken word. Ben had found his faith, but when and where? It still seemed out of character with the man she'd once known.

Seeing Ben so intent on the scriptures forced her to look inside herself. When had she slacked off on her faith? She'd been active in the church until this last year when the committee had gotten so busy with the bicentennial celebration. She needed to get back to participating in her congregation, as soon as the big day was over. She hadn't realized how much she missed the women's Bible study groups.

Her gaze wandered up to the stained glass windows on the sides of the sanctuary, each depicting a different Biblical scene. Her life was going to change drastically when the bicentennial was over. What would her future look like? Were Ben and Charlie a part of it?

Quickly she focused back on the sermon. Those questions were too big to be dealt with today.

Olivia stepped into her office Monday morning, her thoughts churning on a waterwheel of emotions. They rolled between trying to keep her mind off Ben and keep her distance, and wanting to share every little moment about Charlie with him.

The dog was a great idea. He was no trouble and seeing the joy and delight in her nephew's eyes she knew it had been the right thing to do. It left her with another problem, however. How to allow Ben to participate in her and Charlie's life and still keep her heart protected? She had a feeling it was going to be harder than she'd expected.

"Olivia, can you come here please?"

The summons from Delores was a welcome diversion from her tumbling thoughts. She made her way to the office and braced for bad news when she saw her boss's deep frown.

"We have a situation and you're going to have to get on top of it ASAP."

"What kind of situation?" Whatever had happened, Olivia knew it wasn't on her end.

Delores clasped her hands on the desk, a sure sign she was agitated. "Will Huffman has left without any notice. Which means there is no one overseeing the upcoming Bicentennial Brides event. So, I'm putting you and Ben in charge."

Olivia's nerves jumped. She'd forgotten about that event. It was one of the few committees she'd never worked on. For good reason. Dealing with wedding arrangements was the last thing she ever wanted to do again. "How much is left to organize?" Will had

had months to get all the arrangements made. There shouldn't be much left to oversee. "Do we know why he left?"

"No." Delores pushed a thick folder toward her. "Here's his info. I've emailed you his online files but there's not much there."

"What do you mean?"

"It seems Will has been delinquent in his preparations for the big event."

"In what way?"

"All ways. Other than booking the couples and the Riverbank Park, he's done very little toward the planning. I haven't gone through everything but, well, you'll see. I'd like you to get on this now. We have twenty-five couples expecting a special wedding day and we are not going to disappoint them. You and Ben need to tackle this yesterday. Are we clear?"

A knot formed in the center of Olivia's chest. The last thing in the world she wanted to do was work on a wedding assignment with Ben. The mere thought opened the gates on her past pain.

Olivia picked up the folder and heard herself reply with a "Yes, ma'am," but her voice sounded odd to her ears.

Back in her office she flipped through the folder, her anxiety growing with each page. Will had left the bulk of the details untouched. Which meant she'd have to choose the bouquets, the cake, the music.

Her mind filled with memories of making those choices for her own ceremony. She'd labored over each detail trying to create the perfect day. A knot formed in her throat and she choked back tears. How was she supposed to wade through all the wedding preparations with Ben at her side? Memories rushed through her, sending heat and ice racing through her veins. She couldn't do this. No one could expect her to agree. It was too cruel. She recalled her boss's words from the other day. She wasn't the quiet, naive woman of three years ago. She was stronger, more confident. She could separate the past from the present.

"Good morning." Ben breezed into the office. "Sorry I'm late. I saw Delores in the hall. She said we have a new assignment."

Olivia opened her mouth to speak, but the words stuck in her throat, so she nodded and prayed for strength to see this through. She quickly explained the situation to Ben.

He shook his head. "How could someone drop the ball like that? Don't worry—we've got this. We will make it happen."

Olivia nodded. "I know. But it's going to be a lot of work. We're practically starting from scratch and the event is only ten days away."

Ben leaned forward, a puzzled look on his face. "Okay, I have to ask, what in the world is a Bicentennial Bride?"

A memory vivid and painful flashed through her mind. A wedding, a church filled with flowers, a dress that matched the one of her dreams and a bouquet so perfectly arranged she'd cried when she first saw it. It was supposed to be the joining of two people in love, but the love died and the ceremony died with it.

Olivia swallowed the lump in her throat. "It's a special wedding ceremony for twenty-five couples in the Riverbank Park, all sponsored by the bicentennial committee and supported by local businesses."

Ben hunched his shoulders and frowned. "Why would they do that?"

Was he really that unimaginative? "This is a special year, and this will be a wedding they'll all remember as being part of the big bicentennial. Every bride married this last year was designated as a Bicentennial Bride and was given a special plaque. The couples who will be married the weekend before the actual day will too, but they also will receive a bridal bouquet from the florist and each will have a small wedding-cake venue set up for them to use."

"Wouldn't it be better to have your own private event?"

Olivia struggled to keep her tone even and professional. "Many can't afford a huge wedding and this is an opportunity for them to have a very special day to mark the occasion and not cost them. Of course they can all arrange a reception elsewhere afterward, but for the majority, it's more about making the day unique and being part of the history of the town."

Ben looked skeptical. "I think I'd prefer a traditional ceremony in a church."

Olivia's throat closed up. "Apparently not. You didn't stay for your own." She heard his sharp intake of breath but didn't wait for him to speak. She stood and walked out of her office, not stopping until she was outside. She needed to breathe and take time to process this new turn of events.

Away from Ben.

Ben kicked himself mentally for the tenth time for his thoughtless remark about a traditional wedding. He might as well have slapped Olivia in the face. The pain in her voice had sliced through him like a hot knife. When he thought about that day, he only thought about Olivia being alone, in a room, crying or angry or stunned. He rarely thought about the ceremony. It wasn't the main focus. He was quickly learning that he had a lot to learn about weddings and the place they held in a woman's heart.

He might have had a noble intent when he walked away but clearly he'd missed the more important point. Obviously, working on this wedding-planning deal was hard for Olivia. He'd do his best to make it easy for her, but he had no idea how to go about that.

Ben busied himself with work on the souvenir booklet while he waited for Olivia to return. When she entered the office again, she was stiff-backed and unsmiling. He'd come to recognize that posture. She was determined to follow through on the job no matter what. A small swell of pride touched his heart. The sweet young woman he'd fallen for had become a strong, capable woman and he liked the change.

He debated how to approach her. She was seated at the desk focused on a file. Maybe the direct method was best. "Where do we start?"

Olivia rubbed her forehead. "I can't believe this. Will hasn't followed through on anything. The bridal bouquets aren't decided, the cake venues haven't been selected let alone the cakes themselves."

Ben wasn't sure of the importance of that information. "Is that bad?"

"It gets worse. There's no itinerary for that day or for the rehearsal the night before. I have no idea about the minister." She closed the folder and exhaled. "How could this happen? Will has always been so dependable."

"Can we get this thing organized in ten days?"

"I don't know. I'm not even sure where to start."

Ben shook his head. "Don't look at me. You're the one who's planned a wedding."

A deathly silence fell between them. Ben could have cut out his tongue. Why couldn't he remember how important this was to Olivia? She'd gone pale and distant at his thoughtless words. "Livvy, I uh, I didn't mean to…"

She squared her shoulders and stared at the file. "Let's just focus on what has to be done. Nothing else."

"Right. Good idea. Tell me where to start and I'll get it done."

"I don't know yet. I'll need to go over everything and then divide up the tasks." She faced him. "We're going to make this happen and it's going to be everything these brides dreamed of. They signed up for a special day and I'm not going to let them down. You only get one special day like this in your life."

Ben saw the sadness and determination in her dark eyes. He knew she was dreading working with him on this task, but he'd do everything he could to make it the day she wanted. For her sake and for the brides'. "We'll make it special, Livvy. I'll help you. I promise."

He'd meant to encourage her but instead he saw doubt in her eyes. His poor decision three years ago was going to linger in her mind forever.

Olivia took a deep breath and laid her hands on the desktop. "First things first. Check with the justice of the peace, Leroy Hill, and see if he's still planning on officiating. Then get with the park director and see what has been done there. We'll regroup at lunch and see where we are. I should have a better idea on things after I go through Will's notes."

An overwhelming desire to give Livvy a hug hit him but he knew that would be a big mistake. He walked out of the office but stopped and glanced back at his former fiancée. She'd turned her head to the side, her one hand resting at her lips. The sadness in her body language broke his heart.

Somehow, someway, he'd not rest until this

event was everything Livvy wanted. He could never give her back the day she dreamed of, but he could do everything in his power to make this ceremony as perfect as possible.

He would not let her down again.

Chapter Six

By late morning, Olivia had organized the tasks and divided them between her and Ben. She gave him the majority of the legwork and she'd deal with the logistics. She had a feeling, however, that they were going to run into more issues than were apparent at the moment.

No matter what her own emotional toll, Olivia was bound and determined to make this mass wedding everything the brides had hoped for. She knew she could pull it off but only if she and Ben worked separately. Unfortunately, she knew she'd never trust him to do things the way she wanted, which meant she'd have to stay on top of everything if this was going to happen.

Ben returned shortly before lunch. She looked up as he came into the office. His expression mirrored her own emotions. Discouraged and overwhelmed. She sighed. "Tell me some good news."

He shrugged and sat down. "There's one bright spot. I spoke to the justice of the peace, and he can still handle that."

"That's something."

"How are things on your end?"

"Not that great. I've spoken with the vendors and they are irritated because they've been waiting for instructions and details and haven't gotten them. Will didn't follow through on the number of chairs needed for guests at the ceremony or the tables for the cakes, nor the linens and tableware." She rubbed her forehead. "What about the park director?"

"He's still willing to work with us. He has all the info but we need to get over there and designate the location of each cake table. Twenty-five cakes take up a lot of space, which means that a large section of the park will be off-limits to the public on a busy Saturday. I made an executive decision on that. Will had the tables spread out all over the park. I suggested we set them up around the pavilion for quicker access and teardown. I told him I'd check with you though."

Olivia nodded. "I agree. We have to have the wedding cleared out by midafternoon because they have a band coming in to play. The cakes are more of a picture moment than a time to feed the families."

Ben grinned. "So, it's a cut and run thing, huh?"

Olivia scowled. "The cake cutting and feeding to each other is one of the quintessential moments of the wedding. Everyone wants a picture of that."

"I never realized it was such an iconic moment. What's next on our list?"

"I spoke with Mona at the bakery, and she can do some of the cakes. Crawford's grocery has agreed to do ten. I've put in a call to Linda Wheeler, she makes cakes as a small business, and she can do five for that day. Now I have to settle on a design. All the cakes will be the same."

"Why's that? Wouldn't each bride want a special cake of their own?"

She nodded. "If they were hosting their own reception, but this is a one-size-fits-all kind of event. If you let personal tastes get involved, you'll have chaos. Many of the couples will go to private gatherings after the cake cutting. They all understood the process when they signed up."

Ben stood. "Maybe you should cancel the whole thing."

Olivia set her jaw and glared. She'd been expecting this. "Sure. Why not? It's only a wedding after all. No big deal." Ben looked appropriately chagrined.

"I'm sorry, Livvy. I wasn't thinking."

She looked him in the eyes. Why couldn't he understand? "I won't let these brides be disappointed and heartbroken." She clamped her teeth together before she said, *like I was*. This wasn't the time to be at odds with Ben. She needed him.

"What's next?"

"I need you to go to Polly Benedict at Petals and Pails and check the status of the bridal bouquets. She's sure she can fill the order but she needs to know what flowers we want to use. You'll have to tackle that."

Ben rubbed the side of his neck. "I'm not sure I'm the right one to be handling flowers. Aren't the brides each picking out their own?"

"No. There's one design for everyone. The same as the cakes. Allowing the brides to personalize things would be a logistical nightmare." Olivia waved a hand in the air. "This was the committee's idea, not mine. We just have to make it work."

Ben frowned. "And the ladies are all right with that? Seems a bit impersonal. Why would they choose to do their vows this way?"

Surely Ben could grasp the significance of this ceremony? "Like I said, it's a way of being part of local history." She was aware of Ben's gaze upon her but didn't look up. "You better get going."

Ben started to leave. "What kind of flowers should I pick out?"

"Something simple. Polly will know what to use." She checked the time. "Let's meet up at the park at four and see where we are."

She watched Ben leave then cradled her head in her palms. This would be so much easier if she could keep her memories at bay. Talking about cakes and flowers stirred up visions of her meticulously designed four-layer cake and the fragrant bouquet she would have carried.

Shoving aside the past, she focused on making this large wedding as special and meaningful as she possibly could. Even if she had to work around the clock to make it happen.

Allowing old disappointments and pain to get in her way was counterproductive.

Ben parked in front of the flower shop and stared out the window. He'd decided to tackle the least appealing job first. He knew next to nothing about flowers. Especially wedding bouquets. He tried to think back and remember Livvy's bouquet but drew a blank. No surprise. He was beginning to realize how oblivious he'd been to the things that mattered most to her.

He'd winced inwardly. When Livvy had vowed to make the event special and not disappoint the brides, the words *like I was* weren't spoken, but he heard them loud and clear.

After reaching into his pocket he pulled out a peppermint. He was beginning to wonder if he'd ever dig himself out of the deep hole he was in with Olivia. All he could do was remove one shovelful at a time.

The shop was filled with people and more flowers than Ben had ever seen. Polly greeted him and suggested he look around while she helped her customers. The more he looked, the more confused he became. "How do you pick just one?"

"It's not easy."

Ben turned at the comment to find a young woman smiling at him. "I feel a bit overwhelmed and way out of my comfort zone."

She chuckled softly. "I understand. My fiancé has no clue when it comes to flowers."

"Are you here to pick out your bouquet?"

"No. I'm looking for flowers for my parents' anniversary. I'm not sure what our bouquets will look like. They'll all be the same."

Ben's curiosity rose. "Oh, are you one of the brides taking part in that big ceremony?"

She nodded. "It's going to be so wonderful. We'll be part of history for the rest of our lives. I'll be able to tell our grandchildren how we were married during the town's most important day."

"You and twenty-four other couples. Doesn't that take the shine off it for you?"

She looked surprised at the question. "No. My great-grandparents were married in a mass ceremony during WWII. They were married for sixty-eight years. Besides, Derek and I aren't rich. This is a way to have a special day and not go into debt."

Ben hadn't considered that aspect fully. "That's wise."

"We're trying to be responsible, but we still want it to be a special day. A wedding day is the first big life event we'll share together. Everything about it has to be special and memorable."

Ben smiled at the young woman. "Best wishes."

"Thank you."

She wandered off, leaving Ben with a strange knot in his center. Memorable. His wedding day would be a day to remember for Olivia. But not in a good way. His thoughts circled around to that day three years ago and his mindset at the time. How and when had he become so disconnected with the significance of the wedding? How had he missed realizing how important it was to his bride?

He walked over to a display of fragrant flowers. He vaguely recalled seeing flowers in the sanctuary that day and the boutonniere left for him. It was a blue color. None of that had seemed important at the time. He'd messed up. He'd never understood about the details of the ceremony. Nora was right.

He rubbed his forehead. His plan to talk to Olivia and explain himself that day suddenly seemed thoughtless and even cruel. He'd had good intentions but maybe the best thing for him to do was to leave. He'd have to find another way to deal with his guilt.

The echo of Olivia's voice penetrated his dark thoughts. No. The last thing he would do is walk away from her now. He'd agreed to help, to work alongside her until the big bicentennial event was over, and he'd see it through. But being close to her—with his new insight it would be more difficult.

If only he could go back and give her a little of what she'd lost. Polly motioned him to her office and as he walked he got an idea. It was probably crazy but he wanted to try to make it happen.

Olivia unlocked the front door and smiled as Charlie darted inside. They'd been invited to supper at Marcy Jo's. Her nephew had taken a liking to her friend. Marcy Jo was a great cook and the meal she'd prepared was delicious and relaxing and took the edge off Olivia's anxiety over the botched bridal event.

She stepped through the door of her house and realized Charlie was standing still on the carpet, looking down. It took only a second to realize the carpet was soaking wet. A quick search revealed water trickling from the kitchen into the living room.

"Aunt 'Livia, it's wet."

"I know, sweetie." She tiptoed to the kitchen and quickly found the culprit. Water was flowing from the dishwasher, flooding the kitchen and the living room. Stunned, she tried to think of what to do.

After moving quickly to the valve under the sink, she turned off the flow of water. At least she hoped that was what she was doing. Thankfully, the water stopped, but the damage was done. She hated to think how extensive it was. Without thinking, she pulled out her phone and called Ben. She spoke before he could say hello. "My house is flooded."

"What happened?"

"I think the dishwasher broke. The kitchen is flooded, and the living room carpet is soaked. What do I do?"

"Turn off the water."

"I did. But what now?"

"I'll be right over."

Ben stepped inside the front door and stopped in his tracks. "I think you're going to need more than bath towels to soak up this water."

Olivia sighed and dropped the stack of towels in her arms onto the sofa where Charlie was sitting with Rudy. "I know."

Olivia watched as Ben did a quick survey of the dishwasher and the damage. "What do you think?"

"I think you can't stay here. I'm going to turn the water off at the street just to be safe."

"Move out? To where?"

Ben smiled and picked up Charlie. "Aunt Nora's. She's got plenty of room, it's close and she'd love to have you."

"You don't know that."

"Of course I do. You'll see. Pack what you need for tonight. I'll call a restoration company and see how quickly they can get this cleaned up."

Olivia didn't move. Her mind was having a hard time getting signals to her body. She had to leave her house. Worse yet, she had to move in with Ben. Well, Nora actually but Ben lived there, which meant being in closer contact than usual. "I don't know."

"I can take you to the Lady Banks Inn or the motel outside of town."

Visions of Charlie confined in a motel room with all his energy made her shiver.

Not the way she'd planned on spending her evening.

"I'm going to take Charlie and Rudy over to Nora's, then I'll come back to give you a hand."

Alone in her water-soaked home, Olivia fought off discouragement. Her beautiful little bungalow was flooded and it was starting to smell bad. A tear formed in her eye. The carpet had only been down a few months. She walked into the bedroom and realized the carpet in here was damp too.

She had just finished gathering up her belongings when Ben returned. She snapped her suitcase closed, her heart aching. Leaving her little sanctuary was harder than she'd expected.

"Ready to go? Nora is excited and so is Charlie."

"I hope he doesn't get upset by moving. He just got settled here."

"Don't worry about that. Nora showed him his room and he got all excited because it's on the second floor where he can see more." He chuckled. "And it's got bunk beds. He's a great little guy."

"Are you sure your aunt is all right with us staying?"

"Of course, and Charlie will be fine. He's familiar with Nora and her house. She's been watching him for a while now."

"I know."

Ben grabbed her suitcase and the bag of Charlie's toys while Olivia handled her own rolling cosmetic bag.

"I've already spoken to a restoration company, and they'll send someone out first thing in the morning."

"I don't suppose they could come tonight."

"Sorry." Ben opened the gate on the picket fence that surrounded Nora's front yard. "Livvy, you need to realize this might take several days to clean up and even then, you might not be able to move back in right away."

"Why not?"

"Even after they remove the water the rug

will need time to dry and it may never smell the same again. It'll probably have to be replaced. It'll depend on what other damage the water did. It might have seeped into the drywall and down under the floorboards."

The news made her want to cry. "I wasn't prepared to be out of my house so long."

"I promise, Nora will take good care of you both. You may not want to go home after enjoying Nora's brand of hospitality."

Olivia saw the dimples flash in his cheeks and fought back a wave of attraction. Nora might be a great hostess, but being this close to Ben for a long period of time was not a good thing. Not in any universe.

Within an hour, Nora had worked her hostess superpowers and Charlie was settled in his room trying to decide if he was going to sleep in the upper bunk bed or the lower. Rudy was happily curled up on the makeshift bed Nora had fashioned out of an old pillow and a throw and Olivia was feeling at home in the cheery guest room at the back of the house.

At first she was disappointed she couldn't see her little bungalow and keep an eye on it. But she quickly realized that the backyard of Nora's was like a beautiful park. A small pergola near the back fence was covered in thick blossoms of lavender wisteria. A charming wooden bench rested near a small pond inviting everyone to come and rest.

Everywhere she looked was something sweet and charming in the yard. Had Nora chosen this room on purpose to keep her mind off the work needed across the street? If so, it worked.

The sound of Charlie's laughter rose up from downstairs and Olivia decided to join him. As she walked toward the stairway, she glanced at the steps that led to the third floor. Ben's rooms were at the top. At least there was an entire floor between them. But her room's door faced his at the top of the stairs. That seemed a little too close.

Shaking off her uneasiness she went downstairs and found the others in the kitchen eating brownies warm from the oven. Olivia couldn't resist, and Charlie was on his second one.

"Can Rudy have a brownie?"

"Oh, no, sweetheart. Chocolate isn't good for dogs. It makes them sick."

"I'm glad it doesn't make me sick."

Everyone laughed.

Nora enlisted Charlie's help cleaning up, and Ben and Olivia went to sit on the back porch. Olivia took a moment to admire the yard. "This is like a postcard. Did she do all the work herself?"

"No. Uncle Ted did the hardscape, but she designed it and did all the planting. I loved this yard as a kid. My cousins and I had all kinds of adventures here. There are dozens of places to have secret hideouts and trails."

"No wonder Charlie likes coming here every day."

"I think he and Rudy have already had many adventures." He smiled at her. "How about you? Are you going to be comfortable for the time being?"

She couldn't help but smile. "Oh yes. Nora is so sweet, and my room is very peaceful. In fact, this whole house is peaceful."

Ben nodded. "I loved coming here. My brothers would go off to different camps in the summer, but I always wanted to come here. I had two cousins to play with who were close to my age and Nora was more like a mom than mine was. I always wished I could live with them."

"I can understand that. I had my grandma I visited off and on and I was much happier there than at home with my parents. After they split, life with my mom was hectic."

"And Loretta, were you two close?"

"No. We never had much in common and

she was older and a real wild child. It was like she set out to break every rule in the book."

"And you were the quiet responsible one."

"Guilty." Quiet, responsible and dull. "What kind of kid were you?"

"Curious, searching. I was trying to find where I belonged. I didn't fit with the rest of my family, and I didn't understand why."

Olivia nodded and smiled. "Raised by wolves."

"What?"

"That's what a friend of mine used to say about our families. She was from a very dysfunctional family too and she joked one day that we might as well have been raised by wolves for all the love and guidance we received."

The smile on Ben's face softened. "I guess that's something we have in common. I used to think I must have been adopted because I didn't connect with anyone in my family. I'd stand in front of the mirror and try and find ways that I resembled my parents or my brothers, but I could never find anything."

Olivia bit her lip. She had done the same thing on occasion. Ben held her gaze and she sensed a bond forming between them. They'd both had difficult backgrounds and they both had fought to overcome them.

Suddenly uncomfortable, Olivia decided to change the subject. "I think, when I move back to my house, I'll need to turn my spare room into a proper bedroom for Charlie. He needs a real bed and a bookcase, and he definitely needs more clothes."

Ben chuckled softly. "So you think you've got the hang of this parenthood thing after all?"

She smiled. "Maybe. It's more fun than I expected. And more rewarding."

"I agree. I never thought I'd want kids, then when I stayed with my brother and was surrounded by three little rambunctious boys…" He shrugged. "It awakened something inside me I didn't realize was there."

Olivia looked into his blue eyes and saw her own feelings reflected there. "I didn't think I had any mothering instincts, but maybe I do. I am hopelessly in love with my nephew."

And she feared she was becoming hopelessly in love with Ben as well.

And that meant it was only a matter of time before she had her heart broken again.

Ben stood in the door of his third-floor room, looking down the stairs at the door on the second floor. Olivia's room. Their doors were perfectly aligned. If only their lives and their hearts were.

He closed the door and prepared for bed. Stretched out on the mattress he stared at the ceiling, his thoughts replaying the events from the time Olivia had called about her flooded house.

He was pleased that she called him for help and even more pleased that he'd been able to come to the rescue with an instant solution. Having Charlie in the house was like an infusion of joy. His little smiling face made everyone happy. Olivia brought a different tone to the house. She offered a quiet elegance, sweetness and a sense of home.

The whole evening had played out for him like a perfect homey movie. And he wanted to replay it every night. It was an image he'd dreamed about with Olivia. Until he'd allowed doubts and fears to creep into his mind.

He rolled onto his side. For the next few days, he could live a small part of that old dream. He knew Olivia was anxious to get back in her house, but he secretly hoped it would take a little longer than planned so she'd have to stay here near him.

The next morning was anything but a sweet family picture. Charlie and Rudy were up early, running around the house, Nora dropped the plate of pancakes when Rudy skidded into her and Olivia had a call from Delores begging them to come in early to report on their progress.

They decided to ride together to save time. Delores sounded frantic, which had caused Livvy to tense up. He could tell by the way she had a death grip on the steering wheel when they headed to the office that she was stressed. He had a feeling this bride event situation was an emotional minefield for her, and him too. He was anticipating an explosion of long-buried anger and resentment at every turn but so far she was holding up.

He'd mentioned his concern to Nora last night and she'd reminded him that he needed to be totally supportive. His goal was to be the perfect yes-man. Whatever Olivia wanted, he would provide and agree to. How hard could it be? He pinched the bridge of his nose. He had a feeling he was going to find out.

"What do you suppose Delores is up in arms about?"

Olivia shook her head. "Everything."

"Well, it is a lot to get organized in a short time."

"I know, but I have a plan. I've made a list of everything that has to be done in order of importance and urgency. I'm not going to let a single bride down. We are going to make this happen no matter what we have to do. Are we clear?"

"Yes, ma'am."

Olivia smiled. "Sorry. But there are twenty-five brides out there who have been looking forward to this day for a year. It's important."

"I know. And we'll get it done even if we have to work round-the-clock. I'd better give Nora a heads-up."

"We'll do something special for her when it's all done. And Charlie and I will do something too for having us move in."

"You know she's loving you being there." His aunt was in her element taking care of Livvy and Charlie. Being the hostess was her heart's greatest joy.

"I hope so. She is so sweet."

Ben watched her as she steered the car into the parking lot of the bicentennial office.

After grabbing up her satchel she got out and hurried toward the building. Ben smiled, enjoying the sight of her taking charge. It was a side of her he'd not seen until he'd returned to Blessing.

She looked up at him, a small frown creasing her forehead. "Something wrong?"

He chuckled. "Nope. Not a thing." He held the door for her with a salute. For a brief moment he allowed himself to think about what his life would have been like if he'd stuck it out and gone through with the wedding. No, he hadn't appreciated her back then, hadn't appreciated much in life. The last three years had taught him many things but mostly what love was. Real love. Sacrificial love.

"Let's hope the boss lady likes your plan. I don't think I'd like to be on her bad side."

"She will. I'm more worried about what else might have turned up to deal with."

Ben had the same thought, only his was directed at what would come up with his relationship with Olivia and if he could deal with it.

Chapter Seven

Olivia tucked Charlie in the bottom bunk and kissed him good-night. He'd settled on the lower one because Rudy could curl up at his feet. They'd become inseparable and she was grateful for Ben's gifting him with the dog. Turning out the light, she watched him sleeping, her heart filled with an overwhelming affection that was new to her. Looking back, she couldn't remember why she'd feared caring for him. He'd brought so much joy into her life, and she loved the little guy more with each passing day.

Settled in her room, she read her Bible for a while before turning in. She used to read regularly but after the wedding she'd been too angry at God to want to read His word. Having Charlie in her life had shifted her emotions and she once again was finding comfort in the scriptures. After turning out her light she drifted off to sleep thinking about all the cute clothes and toys she'd buy for Charlie once the bride event was over.

The scream brought her fully awake.

She sat up in bed, heart racing, trying to understand what had awakened her. It came again. A yell, loud, long and filled with terror. Fear chilled her blood. It was a man's scream.

Ben?

She waited, paralyzed. The third time the cry was more of a low moan. Slipping off the covers she then went to the door. Should she do something?

Cracking the bedroom door, she saw Nora peeking out of her room, looking toward the stairs and Ben's room. After a few seconds, Nora closed the door.

Olivia looked up the stairs. Was Ben all right? What kind of nightmare could cause such a bone-chilling scream? Should she check on him? No. Not only would it be inappropriate but intrusive.

She closed her door and paced, trying to make sense of the situation. The creak of floorboards drew her back to the door. Slowly she inched it open just as Ben walked past. She watched him go downstairs, wondering if she should follow him. She closed the door. This was not her concern. Whatever was wrong was his business and if he wanted her to know he'd tell her.

She walked toward the bed then stopped. What if he needed a friend? What if he needed comfort? Who wouldn't after a nightmare like that?

Picking up her sweater she then started down the hallway and stopped in Charlie's room to make sure he was still asleep. He'd been oblivious to the noise.

She found Ben in the kitchen, a cup of coffee in front of him on the table, his feet propped up on one of the chairs. He looked older, sad, defeated. What had happened to him? She debated whether to speak or not but the creaky floors in Nora's old house alerted him to her presence.

Ben jerked around, saw her then looked away. "Go back to bed, Livvy."

The pain in his voice ripped through her. She couldn't leave him like this. She walked toward him, intending to pull out a chair, but as she glanced down her gaze fell on his bare ankles and the wide scar visible below his pants bottoms. She gasped. "Ben. What happened to you? How did you get that horrible…" He quickly put his feet on the floor and leaned his arms on the table.

"Ben?" Her mind was spinning with possibilities, all of them bad.

"You need to go back to bed. Sorry if I woke you."

She tilted her head. "You woke the whole house. Well, except for Charlie and Rudy. They didn't stir."

"It's late, Livvy." He stood and placed his cup on the counter then walked out.

She went after him. "Ben, didn't we agree to get to know each other? The good and the bad? I'm here. Ready to listen."

"Not now. It's not a story you'll want to hear." He left, and Olivia felt that empty sensation again.

Would he always do this to her? Walk out, walk away, walk alone?

Ben made it midway up the stairs before he stopped. His therapist had constantly encouraged him to share his experience with others. It was the reason he had found a group as soon as he'd settled in Blessing. He'd also been encouraged to talk to people close to him, those who cared for him and had a right to know.

But was he ready to tell Olivia what he'd been through? What would she think? Would it change the way she saw him?

Right or wrong, he had a strong need to talk to her. He headed back to the kitchen and met Olivia in the doorway. "If you're willing to listen, I have a story to tell you."

Olivia met his gaze, her dark eyes warm with compassion. "I'm willing."

They sat at the table; she sat close enough to touch him. He wasn't sure if that was a good thing or not. Her touch could either send him into hiding or open a dam of emotions he wasn't sure he could control.

"I told you I traveled. I went to Europe to take photographs. I was seriously thinking about being a professional. I met a guy in Berlin who shared my interest and we decided to explore the mountains and perfect our nature photography skills. His name was Davey Wong."

He met Olivia's eyes, relieved to see she was listening intently. "We wandered around the Ural Mountains for months. Then one day we were shooting pictures of the landscape and suddenly soldiers came out of nowhere and arrested us. They said we'd crossed their border illegally. Though we weren't aware of any borders in the area."

Olivia inhaled softly. "Oh, Ben."

"We tried to explain we were just taking pictures—we produced our passports and other documents, but it was no use. They took us to a small town and locked us up. They interrogated us relentlessly. Davey got the worst of it. They accused us of being spies because of all our camera equipment. But they found a Bible in Davey's backpack and that really angered them."

"Wasn't there someone you could call? The embassy or something?"

Ben shook his head. "Over there, you're guilty until proven innocent. There's no one phone call. It was a very small, very isolated village. Looking back I think the mayor was trying to use us to move himself up the political ladder."

"How long were you there?"

"Nine months. It seemed longer. They kept us isolated. I didn't see Davey for two months except in the small interrogation room once in a while. They'd bring us together and grill us about why we were invading their town. There was only one guy who spoke English but not well and we were never sure about what he asked and I don't think he fully understood our responses."

"And this went on for nine months?"

Ben ran his hands along his thighs. "No. I guess they got tired of asking the same questions, so they changed tactics. One morning they put us in a big truck and hauled us out into the hills. Our new jail consisted of two small cells in an old stone building. No furniture, just a dirt floor. They shackled us to the wall and each morning they'd put us in the truck and drive us out into the woods where we'd work all day then back to our cells at night. The only good part was that our cells were only separated by bars so we were together and could communicate freely."

Olivia teared up. "How did you get away?"

"One day a man came, dumped our belongings on the floor, unlocked the chains and told us to go. We went."

"What happened that they set you free?"

Ben shrugged. "We noticed the town was deserted. I don't know why. We got as far away as fast as we could. We found a small town—the people there helped us. Davey wasn't doing well. He wasn't a large man and the rough treatment had taken a toll. We were taken to a nearby hospital but it was too late for Davey. He died." He swallowed and clenched his fists on the table. "It was my fault. It was my idea to hike in those mountains. I found out later that that part of the mountains has several radical splinter groups vying for power. We just happened upon one."

Olivia reached out to touch him and he

withdrew his hand, placed it in his lap. She winced, sending his conscience spinning.

"I'm so sorry. How did you get back home?"

"I finally managed to get through to my dad—he made all the arrangements. But when I got back, I wasn't in a good place emotionally. I couldn't eat, didn't want to be around people."

"The nightmares?"

He nodded. "Flashbacks, drastic mood swings and a big load of guilt. But I did come home with one big gift. Faith. Davey was a believer. He could literally quote the Bible. We used to have debates on the existence of God." He clasped his hands on the table. "But when we were in those cells, Davey got to me. I asked him how he could stay so upbeat and hopeful. He told me that he knew the Lord was on his side, watching him, helping him accomplish what He had given him to do.

"I asked him how he knew God was watching over us and he told me stories of Joseph and David and Paul. I started asking questions and then one day—" he shrugged and smiled "—I believed."

"That's wonderful."

"It changed me. It helped me get through the therapy and counseling and all of the other stuff that comes with PTSD."

"So, that day at the bakery, you didn't have a migraine."

"No. Sorry. I wasn't ready to explain it to you. I never planned to tell you at all."

"Why not?"

He met her gaze. "Why? I had in my head to come back here, see you, and try and make you understand why I did what I did and make peace. My past mistakes were irrelevant. Nothing to do with you and me. But I had to deal with the guilt."

"Over the wedding?"

"And Davey. I couldn't save him. It was my fault."

"Oh, Ben, you're being too hard on yourself. Is there anything I can do?"

He met her gaze, encouraged by the understanding he found there. "No. It's all on me and the Good Lord. Like Davey promised, He's watching over me—I have no doubt."

He reached out and took her hand in his. The contact felt empowering now. "I'm not the same man you knew, Olivia. That man was focused on his own needs. I'm a different person now."

"I can see that. I see it every time you're with Charlie. So, are you getting better? Will you always have the flashbacks?"

"Maybe. I'm hoping to overcome all that,

but I don't know. Jeff didn't want me to come here. He didn't think I was ready to confront the guilt over…us and Davey too."

"Do you regret coming?"

"No. I've got a support system here. Pastor Shields is a wise man and there's a small group I meet with, but I still have a long way to go." He reached for a candy from the dish on the table and held it up. "This is my focus tool. I have several things I do when I feel a flashback coming or when I'm in the middle of one. I also have a verse I recite and a prayer, but this candy usually does the trick. It yanks me back to reality pretty fast."

Olivia wiped tears from her eyes. "Ben, I don't know what to say. I had no idea, I mean, it's an incredible story."

"Not a story. The truth. I'm all about the truth these days. Better get to bed. Sorry I woke you." He stood, taking Olivia's hand. Without warning, she tugged him close and wrapped her arms around him. He closed his eyes, his mind a swirl of old feelings and sensations. Holding her was like being grounded and secure.

She held him for a long moment then finally stepped back. He looked into her eyes and saw a familiar warmth. Hope rose in his chest. Did she still care? Did she still have feelings somewhere deep inside for him?

He braced himself and forced a smile. "Thanks for listening. I'll see you in the morning."

The warmth in her dark eyes dimmed a bit. He knew he was pushing her away but right now he needed space and time to process, and he couldn't do that with her so close.

She nodded, lightly touched his shoulder and walked out of the room, leaving him with an ache deep inside that he wasn't sure would ever go away.

Olivia went downstairs the next morning to find Charlie at the kitchen table eating a waffle and Rudy sitting at his side, hoping for a scrap. She smiled and gave him a hug and the dog a quick pat on the head.

Nora looked up and started to smile then frowned. "Uh-oh. Didn't you sleep well?"

Olivia took her time fixing her coffee. "No. Not really."

"I assume you heard Ben in the middle of the night."

She nodded. "He came down here and we talked. He told me about his ordeal in Europe."

"Good. I've been urging him to share that with you."

Olivia reached out and gently stroked her nephew's hair. Touching him gave her a sense of comfort. "I hate to think of what he went through. I saw the scar on his ankle and I…" Her throat tightened up. "I can only imagine what he didn't tell me." Ben had never said the words *beatings* and *torture*, but she'd inferred them from the tone of his voice.

"It was traumatic." She joined Olivia at the table. "It's taken him a long time to come to terms with it though he still carries a lot of guilt over his friend's death. And you."

Olivia's mind cartwheeled, tumbling between her pain over being jilted and her heartache over what Ben had endured. "You can't really compare the two." She realized that Ben hadn't put in an appearance. "Where is Ben? I hope he's sleeping in."

Nora shook her head. "He's gone already. He told me to tell you he had an early meeting with the park director about the bride event."

"Oh. Right." The big event seemed pointless in the wake of what she'd learned last night.

"I suppose I'd better get to work too. We don't have much time to sort out this mess Will left us."

"Anything I can do?"

"I'm not sure at this point. We don't even have dinnerware for the cake cuttings. Will was supposed to handle that but he dropped the ball."

"What kind of tableware are you wanting? Paper, plastic?"

Olivia picked up her purse and placed her cell phone inside. "I guess at this point I'll take what I can get, but I'd love to have china plates and silverware and wineglasses. It's just a token moment. A picture opportunity, really, to mark the occasion. They'll cut the cake, feed it to each other and then drink an apple juice toast. After that they'll all go to their private receptions."

Nora smiled. "And you want it to be special."

Olivia nodded. "But finding that much good china this late is going to be difficult."

"Maybe not. Give me a number of how many items you need, and I'll see what I can do."

"You know something I don't?"

Nora winked. "I have connections. You go to work. Charlie and I have this."

Olivia's spirits were elevated thanks to Nora's offer of help. Unfortunately, they took a hit when she walked into the office and saw Ben at the computer.

The memory of last night and the things he'd told her flooded her mind and left her feeling awkward and uneasy. What did she say to him? Did she act like nothing had changed between them? Did she mention it or ignore the whole conversation?

Ben glanced up and she saw confusion in his eyes. He'd bared his soul. He must be feeling vulnerable and exposed.

She smiled and went to her desk. For now, she'd ignore last night's revelations. They had a mountain of work to do in a short time. "You're in early. How did it go with the park director?"

Ben leaned back in his chair. "All set. But there's a new wrinkle. He told me nothing has been done on decorations for the pavilion. As of now, the only things going in there are a podium and chairs."

Olivia exhaled. "I can't believe this. Who was overseeing Will's assignments? Why didn't someone notice this stuff wasn't handled?"

"I asked Delores and she said Will had never needed supervision before. He was as dependable as the sunrise. She did find out that Will had learned his youngest child had cancer. Something like that can mess up your mind in a hurry."

Olivia placed her hand over her mouth. "Oh, how awful. I can't imagine. I'm sure planning this event was the last thing on his mind. Literally."

Ben muttered a reply. "But it still has to get done. By us."

"Well, your aunt may have an answer for one of our issues. She's looking into finding plates for the cake tables."

"Good. One less thing to worry about."

She looked at Ben; there were lines in his face. "Didn't you sleep well? You look tired." She wished she'd not asked. He grimaced and turned away. Stupid question. She knew he'd been stressed last night.

"Not particularly." He stood. "I need to get to the park. Where are you headed today?"

Clearly Ben didn't want to talk about last night. "Marcy Jo and I will tackle the pavilion decorations, though I don't know what we can do on such short notice."

Ben smiled. "I know you'll come up with something spectacular."

His belief in her capabilities warmed her heart.

Ben drove to the Riverbank Park, trying to keep his mind on the dozens of tasks he needed to take care of before the weekend, but all he could think about was Olivia and what she thought about the things he'd told her. Did she think less of him? Was that even possible?

Though they'd been getting along well lately, he thanked Charlie for much of that. The little guy gave them a reason to be together. Having them in his aunt's home was even better. Though, the restoration company had completed their work and Olivia and Charlie would be moving back home by the weekend. He'd miss them. There might only be a street separating them but sometimes it felt like miles.

The park director, Ray McDonald, was waiting near the pavilion when he arrived, and Ben greeted him warmly, thankful for the diversion from his troubled thoughts.

"I redrew the layout for the cake tables as we discussed. I think it'll work well."

Ben turned his attention to the drawing, nodding in approval. "That's fine." He smiled and shook the man's hand. "Not that there's time to quibble over details."

As he started toward the car a young man walked slowly toward him from the other end of the pavilion. He looked uncertain and nervous. "Hello. Nice day, isn't it?" Ben said.

The young man nodded then glanced around. "Are you in charge here?"

"No. But I'm connected with the brides event if that's what you mean."

The man shoved his hands into his pockets. "Are you the minister?"

Ben smiled inwardly. "No. Do you need me to find one for you?"

"No. I just... I uh..." He shifted his weight nervously. "Are you married?"

The question stung. He should be. But he'd walked away from that pleasure. "No. I came close once, but." He shrugged.

"What happened?"

Ben almost refused to answer but then he saw the doubt and worry in the young man's eyes. "I left her at the altar." The words, said out loud, ripped through his heart.

"You did? You're very brave."

"Very cruel."

"What do you mean?"

"I hurt my bride deeply. More than I ever expected."

"Did you regret it later?"

"I did. I do."

The man stared at the ground a moment. "Oh. I'm supposed to be married here this weekend—you know, the big bride thing."

Ben was beginning to understand. "Are you having second thoughts?"

"I thought it would be easier doing it this way, none of that over-the-top nonsense. But I'm still feeling…overwhelmed. I don't know. I love her but it's a big step. It's forever."

"What is it you're afraid of?"

"All of it. What if I'm a bad husband? What if I can't take care of her? I don't have a good job yet. That's why we're getting married here. Weddings are expensive."

"They can be." He'd never considered the expense Olivia had incurred. Maybe he should have offered to pay for it. He doubted she would have taken anything from him at that point.

"What if I've made a mistake? What if she doesn't really love me?" He met Ben's gaze. "Did you feel like this before the wedding?"

Ben nodded. "Not about the same things but I worried I couldn't make her happy."

"Maybe I should just not show up. That had to be easier, right?"

"No. It only made everything worse. I saw her again and I realized how deeply I'd hurt her. I had no idea. I regret that."

"I don't want to hurt her. I love her."

Ben put his arm around the man's shoulders. "Then I suggest you talk to her. She might be having doubts herself. More importantly, I think you need to pray about this. Take time to seek His advice."

"Would you pray with me? I don't know what to say."

Ben nodded then laid his hand on the back of the man's neck and lifted up a request for strength, clarity and confidence.

The man shook his hand and departed, leaving Ben with a sense of accomplishment. Is this what it would feel like when he was helping full-time? He hoped the feeling would never end.

"This is going to be a beautiful venue for the big wedding."

Olivia only heard half of what Marcy Jo said. She was watching Ben at the other end of the pavilion, his hand on the back of a young man, heads bowed. Were they praying?

The man raised his head, then Ben shook his hand and stood watching a moment before walking off toward the parking lot.

She wasn't sure what to make of it.

"Where do you want to start, Ollie? Which end should we place the podium?"

Olivia shut questions about Ben down and focused on the task at hand. Between the two of them they drew up a plan for arranging the chairs and which end of the pavilion to position the justice of the peace.

The bigger problem was acquiring the decorations for the pavilion. She and Marcy Jo had set up a workspace on one of the picnic tables in the pavilion and started calling wedding decor vendors with no luck. The irony was so frustrating. They had the funds to provide lavish decorations but no vendors.

Olivia had almost given up hope when a young woman approached them and looked at Olivia.

"Aren't you the bicentennial lady? I saw your picture in the *Banner* newspaper."

"Olivia Marshall. I'm one of them. Can I help you?"

"I'm Dottie Tremont. I just wanted to thank you for this brides idea. It is a real blessing for my fiancé and me."

"You're welcome but I can't take credit for it. The planning committee came up with the idea. I'm just trying to make it work."

Her expression turned to concern. "Oh. Is something wrong?"

Olivia exchanged looks with Marcy Jo. She didn't want to worry the bride. "We have a little hitch in the decorations for this pavilion, but we'll sort it out."

"Oh. I hope so. This is the only wedding Andy and I will have."

Olivia smiled. "Then I'll work doubly hard to make it perfect."

"It doesn't have to be perfect—Andy and I will take care of that part. But I do want it to be memorable. That's why we signed up. What's more memorable than being married during the city's two hundredth birthday? We'll be part of history forever. We can bring our kids to see the plaque in the courthouse. Besides, it's not the dress or the decorations or even the size of a wedding that matters. It's us, me and Andy. We're what makes the day special." She took a seat beside Olivia.

"When I started planning my wedding I was overwhelmed by the list of things the experts said you had to do, and all the things you must have. I mean really, little boxes for the guests to take home pieces of wedding cake. And a special thank you gift for each guest to take home? Who were we trying to impress anyway? So we decided to take the money we would have spent on an elaborate wedding and buy our first home. We haven't found one yet, but we will, and it's a lot more fun house shopping than running round trying to find the exact right shade of ribbon for the table decorations."

Marcy Jo chuckled. "You have a point. I think that's one of the reasons the committee liked the idea. But now it's our job to make it happen." She stood. "And we need decorations."

Dottie glanced between the two of them. "Did something happen?"

Olivia didn't want to worry her, but she didn't want to lie either. "Well, yes. The person in charge of arranging the details of the wedding left without finalizing everything. My assistant and I are having to scramble to get it all ready for Saturday."

"Oh. Is there anything I can do?"

"Do you know a florist who can decorate this huge pavilion on two days' notice?" She chuckled.

"No, but I have an idea. My best friend had a glitch in her wedding decorations last year and she had to improvise. It turned out to be more beautiful than what she'd planned."

Dottie had her full attention now. "What did she do?"

"Ferns. Ferns and candlestands. She had hanging ferns, standing ones, potted ones with candles in between. It was breathtaking."

"I like it but I'm not sure I could find that many ferns to buy in such a short time."

"Oh, she didn't buy them. She rented them.

Oh, and she had ribbons trailing through them too."

"Dottie, you are a lifesaver. I know a nursery in Hattiesburg that could provide plenty of ferns. Thank you."

Dottie smiled. "Really? I feel like I've actually planned part of my wedding." Her phone rang and she gasped. "Oh my."

"Everything okay?"

She nodded. "It's from Madeline's Closet. They just received two wedding gown donations for me to consider. I couldn't afford a dress of my own, so I was going to borrow a friend's, but this would be better." Her expression faded. "I wish my mom could be here to help me choose. She died two years ago."

Olivia's heart went out to the young woman. "I could go with you. You've helped me so I'd like to help you."

"I'd like that. I'll meet you there in about a half an hour."

Olivia watched Dottie walk away then let her gaze travel around the large pavilion. Ferns and candlelight. The rustic structure was beautiful on its own but the simple decorations would only make it more amazing. *"Thank You, Lord, for sending Dottie to me."*

Olivia was late getting to the used clothing store and found Dottie sitting on a bench outside. "Dottie, what's wrong?" She sat next to the young woman and noticed she'd been crying.

"The dresses were both gone when I got here."

"Oh, Dottie, I'm so sorry."

"The lady said both customers were part of the bride event and looking for dresses they could afford." She dabbed at her eyes. "I guess I'll wear my friend's gown but it was too big and not really my style. I wanted something simple and elegant. But, I guess it doesn't really matter what I wear. It's the ceremony that matters."

Olivia wanted to cry for the woman. She knew only too well how important the gown was. An idea formed and she let it grow. "Dottie, I may have a solution. Can you come to my house this afternoon around four? Here's my address."

"Sure, but what for?"

"Just stop by, and we'll see if my idea will work out for you."

Olivia slowly unzipped the vinyl bag later that afternoon and removed the dress inside. The white gown looked as perfect today as it had three years ago. The simple design only needed a veil and a bouquet to show it off. No ruffles or bows and only a small splash of lace. It had fit to perfection and made her feel like a princess.

She held it up in front of her and faced the mirror. It would never be worn by her again but it might make Dottie's day special. With a sigh, she returned the gown to the garment bag and closed it up.

It was time to let go. Meeting Dottie had made her think back on that day with new insight. Next month to the day would have been their third anniversary. Usually, Olivia ignored the day, letting it fade into the next. This year she probably wouldn't have even thought about it but with Ben back in town it had been on her mind frequently.

Now she wondered which had hurt more, Ben jilting her because he didn't love her or having her day in the spotlight ruined. Had she put too much emphasis on the details, the glitz and glitter of the event, and not enough on their relationship?

Ben was right. They hadn't known each other at all. A marriage would have probably ended quickly. She was a different person. He was too. They knew each other better now. They were working well together.

A knock on the door ended her speculation. Dottie entered the house and Olivia quickly explained the disheveled state of her home.

"Water damage, oh, no. How awful."

"I should be able to move back in soon." She motioned Dottie to follow her down the hall. She quickly unzipped the bag to reveal the gown and heard Dottie's soft gasp.

"It's gorgeous. I've never seen anything like it."

"Try it on. I'm pretty sure it'll fit but if not my friend across the street said she'd alter it for you."

Dottie stared at her. "For me? Is it yours?" She reached out and gently touched the silky fabric.

"It was supposed to be. The wedding never happened."

"Oh, no." Dottie took a step back and held up her hands. "I couldn't use your dress."

"Of course you can. It's just been hanging here for three years. I'll never wear it again and I want you to look beautiful on your wedding day."

Olivia finally persuaded her to try on the gown and to their delight it fit. After repeated reassurances, Dottie left with the gown and a huge smile on her face. She was walking toward her car when Ben showed up. He joined Olivia on the porch.

"What's going on?"

She smiled. "Just helping out a friend."

For the first time she felt a sense of peace about that day. Maybe now she could move forward without the memory festering in the back of her mind. It was in the past and it should remain there.

But what was she supposed to do about her feelings for Ben?

Chapter Eight

Ben jogged down the stairs the next morning and turned into the kitchen. Nora was at her usual spot nursing her coffee; Charlie was eating his favorite breakfast of waffles and Rudy was waiting hopefully for a stray piece to fall his way. He gave his aunt a kiss on the cheek. "You are really enjoying having Livvy and Charlie here aren't you?"

Nora grinned. "I am. They've revived my spirit. I'm taking the little guy to the library today. They are having a model train exhibit."

"Where's Olivia?"

"She left early. She said there was too much to do to get ready for tomorrow."

"That's my cue to get going." He poured his coffee and caught sight of the calendar. The date impacted him like a body blow. How could he have forgotten? He'd been too busy, that's how. A small cloud started to build in the back of his mind. He took a sip of coffee and recited his Bible verse. Three times. *"I can do all things through Christ which strengtheneth me, which strengtheneth me."*

"Ben. Are you all right?"

He shook his head. "No. Not today." Nora was at his side, squeezing his arm.

"Hold on, sweetheart. Remember where you are. You're here with me and Charlie. It's all right. You're safe."

Her words helped. He felt her press something into his hand. A peppermint. It did the trick. His thoughts lifted as he unwrapped the candy. The taste chased away the last dark shadow. But he knew from experience that the date would lie heavy on his thoughts all day.

He'd have to be on guard and keep his mood shielded from Livvy. She had a weird radar setting that could read his moods like blips on a screen. He'd often thought that ability would be a nice addition to a relationship. Then again on the days he needed to hide from the world, it could be annoying to the hilt. But having her near to share his struggle would be a blessing.

He checked with Livvy via text and was instructed to go directly to the pavilion.

Many of the couples had volunteered to step in and help with the setup. With all the helping hands, the chairs were positioned, the cake tables arranged and the podium in position.

The ferns and candlestands arrived on time and Livvy and Marcy Jo had the pavilion looking like a movie set in short order.

Thankful for the hustle and bustle, Ben took a moment to step back and look at the venue. A few days ago he'd doubted if the bride event would even happen, yet now it looked like all that was needed were the happy couples.

Olivia came toward him, and he smiled. He couldn't help it. When he looked at her, she made him happy. He felt like a kid with his first crush.

"Everything is looking good," Ben said. "All we need are the brides and grooms."

She frowned and glanced over her shoulder. "We need a little more. The cake tables are bare. Nora said she had someone to help but I don't know who."

A panel truck pulled up and a tall well-built man got out. "Are you Olivia? I have boxes of dishes, crystal, linens and other things. I'm Luke McBride. My wife, Sara, told me to bring them to you for the cake tables."

Olivia clasped her hands in front of her chin. "Bless you. That's the last piece."

Ben and Luke started to unload the truck while Olivia called for reinforcements.

By midafternoon all the items were positioned on the tables, ready to be set out the next day. Ben's heart swelled with affection when he watched Livvy at work. She loved what she was doing. The more he was around her, the more he realized how amazing she was. Somehow, he and Livvy had managed to get all the details worked out and everything in place. He checked his phone and the date popped up again and he steeled himself against the memory. There was still a lot to do before tomorrow, like the rehearsal this evening. He had to keep busy, keep his mind off the date. Davey's birthday. His mind filled with the memory of how they had celebrated and the cloud started to form again.

The only thing left for today was the rehearsal and the wedding coordinator would handle that. He sat down to wait for Olivia when his mood suddenly took a tumble. He'd avoided thinking about the date but now it rushed back into his mind and pulled him down.

"Ben, I think we should head over here early tomorrow. We still have to arrange the tables' settings, and I want to be there in case the cakes and flowers arrive early."

Her voice came to him from a distance. It took effort to force his mind back to the present. "What?" He turned and faced her. She had a frown on her face.

"What is it? What's wrong?"

He blinked and rubbed his forehead. *Think, Ben, think.* "I'm fine. Just tired. It's been a wild week." She studied him a moment. He knew she wasn't satisfied with his answer.

"Okay. Well, I was saying I thought we should be here early tomorrow just to be on top of things."

"Sure. Probably a good idea. I'll see you at the house." Ben fought his dark thoughts as he headed toward his vehicle. All he had to do was get through today. Tomorrow would be easier. He climbed into his car and stared out into the distance, paralyzed with old memories. He should go home, see Charlie and Rudy and play with them a while. That always cheered him up, but that took effort and at the moment he had zilch.

Someone tapped on his car window. Livvy. He lowered the glass.

"Ben, what's going on? Are you having trouble with the PTSD? Can I help?"

The word *no* was on the tip of his tongue,

but then he looked into her dark eyes and knew she was exactly what he needed. He'd already opened the door to his past, might as well share a little more. "Get in. We can talk." She hurried over to the passenger door and climbed in, her hand landing instantly on his forearm, her gaze meeting his.

"I'm here."

Yes, she was. And he wanted her here, beside him forever. "Today is a rough day for me. It's Davey's birthday."

"Oh?"

"We celebrated his birthday in cells, chained to the wall, but it was a great day."

"What happened?"

Ben chuckled. "We sang hymns. Davey taught me six new ones. He knew every verse of every one."

"That sounds wonderful."

"It was. But the next day was ugly again. So, when this day comes around I remember and I think about Davey and how I should have…" He gripped the wheel. "Well, it's just a tough day, you know."

"I do. I get that way every May twenty-third."

"Oh? What happened…" He growled in his throat and closed his eyes. That was supposed to have been their wedding anniversary. "Livvy, I never meant to…"

She pressed her fingers against his lips. "No. I just wanted you to know that I understand what you're feeling. I didn't mean to make you feel guilty."

He took her hand and held it. Drawing comfort from the connection. His heart filled with regret that he'd walked away from having this kind of comfort every day.

The wedding day dawned clear and sunny with balmy temperatures exactly as Olivia had hoped. So had her special day three years ago, but it had ended with dark clouds of disillusionment. Shoving the sad thoughts aside, she turned her mind to the things that needed to be done this morning. She chose a simple blue dress to wear. She wanted to look professional but not call attention to herself. Today was all about the brides.

An hour later, she was downstairs fixing a cup of coffee. Nora made a good strong brew but secretly Olivia missed the coffee from her own little pot. Thankfully, she and Charlie could move back into the house tomorrow. She'd had to replace the carpet but nothing else was damaged.

She leaned against the counter as she

sipped her coffee. She would miss Nora. She'd spoiled her and Charlie rotten. She couldn't deny that having everyone together was a nice feeling, especially in the evening when she came home. She refused to admit that she'd miss having Ben so close. After all, he was only across the street.

As if hearing her thoughts, Ben appeared in the kitchen. "Are you ready to roll?"

Olivia had to smile at his cheery disposition. Despite his struggle with PTSD, he usually had an upbeat attitude. "I am."

Nora called to Charlie. "Come say goodbye to your mama and Big Ben—they have to go to work."

Charlie and Rudy dashed into the room and went right to Ben. Charlie ran to her next, hugging her waist. "I love you, Aunt Livvy."

Her heart puddled and she bent down and kissed him. "I love you too, Charlie." She'd never expected to feel this way. All she wanted to do was stay home and be with her nephew. Her main focus these days centered around him, not her work. It was a big shift.

When Ben and Olivia pulled up at the park pavilion, they were relieved to find dozens of park employees and volunteers setting things up. It was one of the reasons Olivia loved

Blessing. Everyone was always ready to jump in and help.

A half hour before the ceremony the cakes arrived and were positioned on the tables, then covered with decorated tulle to await the cutting. Olivia smiled at the image the tables made surrounding the pavilion. The ferns were in position and volunteers had added extra touches of ribbon and lights. The effect was stunning.

The florist van pulled up and Olivia went to meet it. If the flowers looked as good as the cakes it would be a successful day. She lifted the first one out and gasped softly. The bouquet was white roses with violets in the center and lavender and sparkle ribbons trailing down in front. This was her bouquet. The one she'd held that day. The one she never got to toss.

She sensed someone come up behind her.

"Did I get it right?"

She turned to face Ben, who had an expectant look on his face. "Did you do this?" He nodded. "How did you know?" She held the bouquet close to her chest and gently touched the flowers in the center of the arrangement, her emotions spinning. She was surprised, happy and touched all at the same time.

"Polly told me." He reached down and

took her hand. "I'm sorry you didn't get to enjoy your special cake and flowers. I thought maybe I could make it up to you in a small way by giving all the brides one like yours. I hope I didn't make things worse."

Olivia's eyes grew moist. She'd never expected such a sweet gesture from Ben. He surprised her at every turn. She inhaled the fragrance of the flowers and met his gaze. "No. It was a sweet thought. Really. Thank you." She leaned forward and kissed him on the cheek, her mind awhirl with memories of them together.

He held her gaze a long moment then held up his hand, one finger pointing at her. "I'm glad but we'd better get to work. Oh, and one of the bouquets is for you. If you want it."

She nodded. Her gaze fell on the flowers again. Maybe Ben was truly sorry after all. Before she realized it, the first notes of the "Wedding March" began to play. The justice of the peace took his place at the lectern and smiled.

Arm in arm, the couples began the slow walk down the length of the pavilion to their places in the front. Olivia smiled at the sight. It was heartwarming to see so many couples committing their lives to one another. The couples all looked so happy, so hopeful. She prayed they'd know the joy of long happy marriages. She hadn't seen that in her parents, but her grandparents had been devoted to each other for over fifty years. That's the image and hope she held in her heart. She wanted to experience the growing up and growing old together, with the same goals in mind, the same values embraced and the same love binding them together over any obstacle that crossed their path.

Her gaze found Ben, who was walking back to the pavilion from making a final check of the cake tables. He smiled. Her heart thudded in her chest. A mental picture formed in her mind of him in a tux, waiting at the end of the long sanctuary aisle, with that same smile. She'd envisioned it a million times in her mind. It never happened.

Olivia absently touched her bouquet as she watched the couples taking their vows. Thankfully, the wedding organizer was in charge today, leaving her free to enjoy the ceremony.

The large ceremony went off without a hitch, all the brides were beautiful and the twenty-five couples were now part of Blessing history forever. Dottie looked stunning in her gown and any lingering doubts about giving up her wedding dress vanished. Before she realized it, the venue was being taken down and the park restored to its normal state.

Ben approached, his camera dangling from the lanyard. "It went well, don't you think?"

"It did. There were times when wrangling twenty-five couples seemed impossible but it was a lovely, memorable event."

"That's what you were going for. A unique, memorable wedding day." Ben touched her arm. "You've made many people happy today. You should be proud of yourself."

"This ceremony wasn't about me."

"I know. I know this has been hard for you. It has for me too. Do you have any idea how many candies I've eaten since we took over?"

She looked at him. Had he really struggled with the memories? He'd already admitted his heavy load of guilt over leaving her. She didn't have an answer. Not yet.

"Delores texted me how pleased she is. When the boss is happy, we're happy."

"I want you to be happy, Olivia. I only wish I could go back and do things differently."

She picked up her bouquet from the bench. "We can't but we can move forward."

Ben smiled. "I'd like that."

Somehow, she and Ben had worked together to make the Bicentennial Brides Event a success. She wondered if they could always work this well as a team. It would be nice to have someone to help her raise Charlie and share her life.

With the ceremony over, she could concentrate on moving back into her little house. She'd missed it, but she'd miss the family feeling she had at Nora's. It was time to regain control of her life.

In a week the bicentennial celebrations would be over and that meant Ben would be leaving. She'd dreaded working with him at first and yet the time had passed quickly. She realized with a jolt that she wasn't ready for him to go.

There was only this week in which she could strengthen her barriers and prepare Charlie for Ben's departure. She bit her lip. She had no idea how to go about that. How did you explain to a four year old that his best buddy wasn't going to be there to play with him anymore? It was particularly difficult when that child had already experienced his mother disappearing.

She would have to work three times as hard to make her little guy feel loved and safe. Ben or no Ben.

Ben pulled to a stop in Nora's drive after church the next day and looked out his rearview mirror at Livvy's charming little bungalow, wishing that was the home he was coming to. He got out of the car and jogged across the street. At least he knew he'd be welcome in her house. He'd have to be content with that.

The door opened as he topped the porch stairs. Charlie raced toward him, hugging him around his knees. "Hi, Big Ben." Rudy joined in, his tail wagging rapidly.

"Hey, little buddy." He picked him up, held him tight, reveling in the feel of the little arms wrapped around his neck. Olivia came to the door, a warm smile lighting her face. Ben's heart skipped a beat. He saw his dream in front of him, but it was out of his reach. Like seeing happiness in a snow globe but doomed to be forever barred from entering.

Olivia motioned him inside. "I didn't expect to see you today. I thought maybe you were wanting some alone time."

He followed her in, lowering Charlie to the floor. "No. I've had enough of that for a while. I stayed after church to talk to Pastor Shields. He's a wise man."

"And you needed wisdom today?"

"Always. Along with that, your willing ear is always welcome, though I promise not to unload on you anymore."

She looked him in the eyes. "I don't mind. It's what friends are for."

His heart skipped. "Are we friends now?"

"Of course. I don't have any bad feelings anymore."

A rush of relief surged through him. "Does that mean you trust me again?"

A shadow passed over her eyes. "I'm getting there."

"I'll take it." He fought to keep from taking her in his arms. She was dressed in jeans and a loose shirt today but yesterday she'd glided around the bride event in a blue dress that did strange things to his system. Every move sent his heart fluttering.

"Big Ben, want to see my new book? Miss Nora got it for me at the liberry."

Ben eased into the armchair and reached for the boy. "Sure. Let's read it." Having the little guy settled in his lap as he read about the little green excavator created a sense of permanence Ben had always longed for. He belonged here, with Charlie and Olivia. If only he could make it come true. Olivia might be learning to trust him again, but there were still too many things between them. Her doubt and his guilt.

Ben was on his third book and a game of race cars when his phone rang. He was expecting it to be the pastor, but his pulse thumped when he saw his brother's name on the screen. He excused himself and stepped into the kitchen.

"Jeff, what's up?"

"Are you somewhere you can talk?"

The tone of his brother's voice sent a shiver down his spine. "Yeah, what's happened?"

"I got a call a short while ago from Davey's parents. They would like to talk to you."

The room spun for a second. The thing he'd dreaded might be about to happen. "Did they say why?"

"Well, they have questions about their son's death and about your captivity."

Ben fisted his hands. "What did you tell them?" There was a long silence before his brother answered.

"Ben, I gave them your cell number. You need to talk to them. I know you don't want to, but you've put it off too long."

His brother was right, but he hadn't been strong enough. He wasn't sure he was yet.

"Yeah. I know."

"And, Ben, they want to come to Blessing to see you in person."

Ben faced the wall and pounded his fist against the surface. "I can't do that."

"Ben, I tried to divert them, but they aren't

backing down this time. You need to face this and get it behind you. I expect they'll be calling you soon—I'm sorry. I know this is hard."

"Yeah. Okay. Thanks. I'll talk to them."

"When you do, let me know. You know you're welcome here anytime. Why don't you come back and take time to heal up?"

"Thanks, bro. I'll let you know how it goes." Ben ended the call, his thoughts spiraling in a dizzy swirl.

Olivia came into the kitchen, her eyes widening when she looked at him. "Ben. Are you okay? What's happened?"

He didn't want to tell her, didn't want to face the family. He didn't want to relive those months. Not with anyone.

"I'm afraid I have to go. I can't stay here. Sorry, Livvy."

"Why?"

He shook his head and walked out, not even saying goodbye to his little buddy. He went to his car, got in and drove. He found himself at the Blessing Bridge Prayer Garden, not sure why he'd come.

He stopped at the top of the curved bridge and grasped the railing, praying for guidance and strength. He exhaled a pent-up breath. It was time to take the next step. Each one along the way had been difficult, but the Lord had upheld him through every moment and He would for this next hurdle. He'd learned there was no going around difficult trials. He couldn't go around it, or past it or run away from it. The only way was to go through and find peace on the other side. Heart beating like a tribal drum, he fought the rising fear and dread swirling in his chest making it hard to breathe. He didn't want to do this. Facing Livvy had been hard enough: facing the Wongs was too much to deal with.

He needed to talk to Pastor Shields again, but he suddenly realized that there was only one person he wanted to help him face Davey's parents.

Olivia. But he'd just told her he wouldn't unload on her again. "That's what friends are for." Dare he test her statement?

He just had to find the courage to ask her. He'd give it time. Maybe he'd be ready to face this meeting after he'd had time to think things through and pray a lot.

Olivia pulled to a stop in front of her house later the next day, relieved to find Ben and Charlie playing fetch with Rudy in Nora's front yard. She bit her lip. Ben was still here. He'd left so suddenly and with no explanation yesterday morning that her old fears had kicked in. Especially when she'd been unable to reach him. She told herself to stop thinking the worst, but she still had that nagging question in the back of her mind. When would he leave again?

Now, as she watched Ben and her nephew together, she prayed that Ben would want to stay, if for no other reason than to be close to Charlie. They had a special bond, one that she suspected Charlie deeply needed.

She stopped at the picket fence that encompassed the front yard and waved. Ben tossed the ball then joined her.

"Everything okay at the office? Sorry I didn't come in today, but I had errands to run, several personal things to take care of."

"It's okay. Today was mostly taking grateful calls from the happy couples or their families. We made their wedding day special, Ben. That's all I ever wanted."

"I know."

"Hey, Big Ben, the ball is stuck under that bush and Rudy can't get it. Hi, Aunt 'Livia. I missed you."

She never tired of hearing that or of seeing her nephew play. Every day he took up a larger part of her life and her heart. As nervous as she'd been at first, now she couldn't imagine her life without him. Olivia bent over the fence and ruffled his hair. "I missed you too."

Ben rejoined them and handed the ball to Charlie, who squatted down and began a serious conversation with Rudy on the best way to retrieve the ball. She exchanged smiles with Ben. "He is constantly entertaining. I never knew children could be so…"

"Lovable?"

She nodded.

Ben turned his gaze to the little boy. "The little fella is special. I don't know how his mom could be away from him for more than a second."

"Me either. Though my mom always made having children sound like a burden that would ruin your life."

"Is that how you feel?"

"Not now. I can't believe how much I adore that sweet child."

Ben held her gaze. "I'm glad to hear that. Do you remember that night after the party for that buddy of mine, we had a little too much to drink and we both confessed that kids were not in our vision for the future?"

Olivia looked away. "I do."

"I don't feel that way anymore. I think, no, I *know* that someday, I'd like to be a father. I'd like several little Charlies in my life."

She nodded. "Me too. Having Charlie here has changed the way I think about a lot of things."

"Aunt 'Livia, I found a big rock. Come see."

Ben opened the gate, and they joined the boy at the edge of the yard. A large flat rock peeked out from under a blooming azalea.

"It's huge." Charlie smiled, his eyes bright.

Olivia stooped down and brushed away the dirt and branches. The rock was about eight inches long, five inches wide and flat. Perfect for painting on. "Charlie, how would you like to turn this rock into something special for the town's big birthday party?"

He nodded enthusiastically. "'Kay."

Ben grinned. "That's a great idea. I'm sure Aunt Nora has craft paint we can use."

A short while later the three of them were on the back porch with paint and three freshly cleaned rocks and were decorating. Olivia took a moment to imprint the moment in her heart. Thanking the Lord for this time with Ben and Charlie, and asking for more. It wasn't in her nature to be greedy, but she enjoyed her nephew so much; each day she thought of more things she'd like to share with him.

And Ben.

Olivia painted a picture of the porch swing,

her favorite spot. Ben's rock displayed a crude rendition of the Blessing Bridge.

"Are you done, Charlie?"

"Yep, I mean, yes, ma'am."

She moved to the end of the table, glanced over his shoulder and caught her breath.

"I made a picture of my house."

He'd painted a house, blue with a porch and steps. It was obvious that Charlie's "house" was Olivia's little blue bungalow. Her heart squeezed and tears stung her eyes.

"It's beautiful, Charlie. You did a great job."

"Can we take it to the park so everyone can see it?"

"Of course."

Ben took her hand. "I think Charlie is happy with you. You've given him a home."

"It makes me wonder what kind of life my sister had given him. He's only been here a short time, but he's changed so much."

"I know. It's amazing." He squeezed her fingers. "That's what love can do. It changes everything. Especially people. I learned that in Europe. All the pain and fear and in the middle of that I discovered what real love was and it changed me. Forever."

Olivia thought about all that Ben had been through and her heart warmed. She placed her hand on his cheek. "You're a good man, Ben."

"Can we go now? My paint is dry."

"Of course."

Charlie fell asleep on the way back from the park. They'd left his rock at the collection center where they'd treat it to preserve the picture. Charlie wanted to put his rock in the park right away and she'd had to explain that they must wait for others to do their rocks.

It had been a sweet and memorable time. Ben had taken dozens of pictures to preserve the moment and to capture the look of joy on Charlie's face forever.

Olivia wanted to remember it too. She wanted to capture the expression on Ben's face as he interacted with her nephew. His whole demeanor changed and became softer and gentler. She liked that Ben. A lot.

That Ben was a man she could love forever.

Chapter Nine

Ben entered his room the next morning and tossed his phone on the dresser only to have the Call Alert sound. He glanced at the screen and froze. Henry Wong, Davey's father. The call he'd been dreading since his brother had phoned. For a second, he considered not answering. He'd avoided this for years. It was time to face up to what he'd done.

His chest tightened. Thankfully the call was short and to the point. Davey's parents would be in Blessing next week. He was facing several days of anxiety. Talking to them would be the hardest thing he'd ever have to do. In many ways, harder than talking to Olivia.

Moving to the window, he looked out at the house across the street. The only thing that would make the meeting tolerable would be if Olivia was there as moral support. He wasn't sure he had the courage to ask for her help. This was his burden to bear, not hers.

Maybe now was a good time to go to Jackson and take care of the next phase of his life. A few days away from Livvy and Charlie might give him the perspective he needed. The Wongs would be arriving on Tuesday. Keeping his mind on something other than the bicentennial would be a more productive use of his time.

Though, his future was another topic he'd yet to share with Olivia. Clasping his hands behind his head he closed his eyes. *"Lord, will my life ever be normal again? Will the past hold me captive forever?"*

He made the decision in an instant. After pulling his duffel from the closet he stuffed in what he'd need for the next few days. He pulled out his phone and typed a text to Livvy then shoved the phone into his pocket. He should speak to her in person, but if he did, he'd lose his courage. He had to take care of things in Jackson.

Inside his vehicle, he looked out the rearview mirror at Olivia's house. All he wanted to do was stay here and be near her and the boy. But his life was already moving in a new direction. Staying in Blessing had never been on his radar. In one week the bicentennial would be over and he'd be out of a job. One week after that he had to report to class.

He was on the highway when a call from his brother came through. "What's up, Jeff?"

"You in your car?"

"Yeah. I'm heading to Jackson to take care of a few things."

"Did you hear from the Wongs?"

Ben's mouth went dry. "Yes. They're coming to Blessing on Tuesday."

"And?"

"And what?"

"You want me there? You need someone with you. I don't like the idea of you meeting them by yourself. What if they get angry or upset?"

Ben had the same thoughts, but he'd reminded himself that whatever transpired, they deserved to know about their son. He'd have to rely on the Lord to give him the words to say at the time. "I'll be fine. I'll let you know how it goes."

"Are you sure? Baton Rouge isn't that far away, and I don't mind coming up there."

Ben appreciated his brother's concern but sometimes being the youngest made his older brother think he was incapable of doing anything on his own. "Jeff. I've got this. I'm not alone. I've got a friend in a high place."

Jeff grunted. "I know. Sorry. Just, well, take care of yourself, okay?"

"I will. Love ya, bro."

Strangely his brother's call had revved up his resolve. He could meet the Wongs and answer their questions.

Though it would be nice to have Livvy at his side.

He's gone.

Olivia scolded herself for that thought. Hadn't Ben proved that he wasn't going to suddenly give up and disappear? But something was wrong. She'd arrived at work this morning to learn that Ben had taken time off for personal time.

What did that mean? Why hadn't he told her he was leaving? She quickly scanned her messages but there was nothing from Ben. No text, email, nothing. Was he having PTSD issues? If so, why hadn't he come to her? She could have helped him somehow. But not if he just disappeared. *Like before.*

She remembered the phone call he'd received at her house and his abrupt departure. It had left her with a bad feeling. She sensed him pulling away and that unleashed her deep fear again. Maybe he'd decided to move on, though he still had the big birthday event to photograph.

After pulling up her list, she scanned the two columns. As Marcy Jo had predicted, the Good column was longer than the Bad. She read all the things she'd learned about Ben. Surprisingly, she hadn't added to the list lately. They'd been too busy with work and enjoying being together.

A small knot formed in her chest. She wasn't ready for him to leave. Still, she couldn't shake the strong feeling he already had one foot out the door. She'd texted him but he'd not responded. Where was he? Why hadn't he told her he was taking time off?

Marcy Jo walked in and laid a stack of mail on her desk. "Do you have any idea why Ben took time off?"

"No. Why?"

Olivia frowned. "He didn't tell me, and I can't get in touch with him. He's not answering my texts or calls. I think his phone is turned off."

Marcy Jo waved off her concern. "Maybe he needed time off the grid." She huffed out a breath. "I could use time hiding away."

"I know, but why, and why didn't he tell me?" Irritation took hold. She set her jaw. "This is what he does—he just disappears without a word, leaving behind a mountain of questions."

"To be fair, he only did that once."

Olivia glared at her friend. She was in no mood to hear facts. Marcy Jo held up her hands in surrender.

"Sorry. I know it was a big deal, but I think he's a good guy. I like him and I know he's in love with you. And—" she grinned "—I suspect you've never stopped loving him."

She shoved the mail aside. "Well, you're wrong. On both counts. People who care about one another don't disappear without explanation or warning. That's a coward's way out."

"I'm sure he'll turn up soon."

Olivia bit her lip. Her old fears were coming to life again. "He's left, hasn't he?"

Marcy Jo spun around. "No. Of course not. Why would you think that…oh, sorry. Right. But no, I don't think he's left. He's just…busy. At least give him a chance to explain. Have you talked to Nora?"

"She's in Atlanta, visiting her son."

"I guess you'll have to wait until he gets back. I'm sure he'll have an explanation."

Olivia pursed her lips together. He always did.

Two days later, Olivia sat on the porch

swing watching Charlie and Rudy play on the porch and enjoying the soft twilight breeze, though not as much as she usually did. Over the last forty-eight hours she'd gone through a catalog of emotions, everything from fury and anger to worry and concern and finally into disgust and a determination to never speak to Benton Kincaid again.

At this moment, however, she just missed him. Pure and simple.

Charlie came and climbed up on the swing beside her. "Aunt 'Livia, where's Big Ben? I want to show him the picture I made for him."

"On a trip, sweetheart."

"Where did he go? I wish he was home with us."

The image that swooped into her mind pricked at her emotions. She wished that too. She felt the most content when they were together in her cozy living room, watching Charlie play and Rudy snuggled up beside Ben. The way she'd dreamed about three years ago.

"I'm sure he'll be home soon."

Charlie snuggled closer and laid his head on her shoulder. "Are you my mommy now?"

Every part of her being warmed with joy and love. If only she was his mother. She hugged him close and kissed his head. "No, you have a mommy. But I can be your favorite aunt."

"I love you, Aunt 'Livia."

Tears stung her eyes. "I love you too, Charlie."

"And Rudy too?"

"Yes, and Rudy too."

And Ben. The thought struck home. She was falling in love with him again. No, she'd never stopped. She'd hoped those lingering feelings would disappear but working with him had only ignited them again.

After putting Charlie to bed she opened her Good and Bad list and started to scan the entries. With a loud sigh she closed the laptop again. There was no use. She knew exactly what was on the list. Maybe it was time to think about what wasn't. Like his thoughtfulness in duplicating her wedding bouquet for all the brides to use and one just for her. The way he was always there when she needed him.

And as far as being trustworthy, he'd never failed to show up or do his job.

So why was she still holding on to her fear?

It was almost dark when she saw his car pull up in Nora's driveway. Her emotions bounced between anger and relief as she watched him get out of his car and turn to stare at her house. He looked tired and tense. Something was wrong. She thought about all he'd endured and berated herself for being so judgmental.

Quickly, she went to her front door and opened it. He bowed his head a moment then started forward. She waited until he was inside the living room before speaking.

"What happened? Charlie's been asking for you. You disappear for two days and don't even tell me? I've been worried sick."

"I sent you a text."

She shook her head. "No. There was no text. You didn't answer any of my messages or voice mails either."

He quickly scanned his messages, and exhaled heavily. "Sorry. I wrote it but never sent it." He rubbed his forehead. "Something came up and I needed time to think it through."

The pain in his voice chased away all her irritation. "What? What's happened?"

Ben sank down onto the sofa. "I honestly don't know. Maybe not."

She curled up on the sofa beside him. "Please. Tell me what's going on."

Ben reached for her hand. "I got a call from Davey's parents. They want to meet with me."

She didn't grasp the significance of his words. "Is that bad?"

"Yes. I've been avoiding them since the day Davey died."

"Why?"

"How do you tell a man's parents that he died because of you? I knew they would blame me, hate me. I wasn't strong enough to deal with them when I got home and after a while, I just ignored the whole situation. Then a week ago, Jeff got a call from them. They wanted to meet with me. He gave them my number. I've been on edge since then, waiting for them to call."

"And they did?"

He sighed and squeezed her hand. "Last Sunday, when I was at your house."

"You should have told me."

He shook his head. "I'd just promised that I wouldn't unload on you again."

"And I told you I was your friend and willing to listen."

He touched her cheek. "After what I did to you, how can you even look at me? Sometimes I wish you'd just haul off and sock me one."

She giggled. "Not sure that would solve anything. Besides, that's in the past, Ben. We need to leave it there."

He shook his head. "The past is always there. Reminding you of your mistakes and your failures." He worked his jaw.

She had a feeling he wasn't talking about their past. The pain in his eyes told her how worried he was. "Are you going to meet with them?"

He nodded. "They want to talk to me about our time in captivity."

"You talked to me."

"That was different. The Wongs are coming to confront me about why I didn't save their son."

"You had nothing to do with that. Surely they know that." He faced her, his expression clearly revealing his torment.

"But I did. It was my idea to hike in that area. Davey wanted to photograph a village he'd heard about, but I wanted to get shots of the forest. There was a contest for landscape photos, and I thought I had a good shot at winning. It never occurred to me that we could encounter a group of radicals in those mountains."

"That's not your fault. Why do you think they want to blame you?"

"Why wouldn't they? We went through a lot, and I came out alive and Davey didn't. If the situation was reversed, I'd demand an explanation."

"When are they coming?"

"Early this week."

"They're coming here to Blessing?" Olivia realized how serious the parents must be. No wonder Ben was anxious.

He arched his brows. "They want to talk to me in person. That doesn't sound good, does it?"

She tried to think positively. "Not necessarily. Maybe they just want to be close to the last person to be near their son."

"Or maybe they're bringing an attorney."

"For what reason?"

"I don't know." He leaned forward, resting his elbows on his knees, his hands clasped beneath his chin. "I'm dreading this meeting, but I need to face this part of my past. I can't put it off any longer."

She hated seeing him in such distress. It wasn't like the Ben she knew. "I could come with you for moral support." She'd expected him to refuse, but he met her gaze, his eyes reflecting hope.

"I can't ask you to do that."

"You're not. I'm volunteering. If you don't want me beside you, I can at least be in a room nearby."

"Are you sure?"

"Of course. Where are you going to meet them?"

He met her gaze and there was an expectant look in his eyes. "I'd like to meet them here, if you're okay with that."

She reached over and took his hand. "My house is fine. Try not to worry. I doubt if they are coming all the way from…"

"Oregon."

"Oregon to grill you about why their son died and you didn't." Ben didn't look convinced but he squeezed her hand. She had a flash of memory; being on the same page again felt good.

She just couldn't forget to be cautious where Ben was concerned. Like Ben said, the past was always there to remind you of your mistakes, and trusting Ben again could be a big mistake.

Thankfully, the next few days went quickly. With the big two-hundredth birthday event looming there was plenty to keep her and Ben busy along with finalizing the souvenir booklet. Unfortunately, today was filled with tension. The Wongs were due this afternoon and no matter how hard she tried to concentrate on work, her thoughts kept going back to Ben. He was out taking pictures in the morning, but when he arrived at her house after lunch, he looked more stressed than she'd ever seen him.

On impulse she went and gave him a hug. He clung to her and she found herself wishing the moment would go on forever. She pushed out of his embrace and held his gaze. "It'll be all right, Ben. You can do this. And I'll be right here for you."

An hour later, Ben was growing more tense. He was pacing and literally wringing his hands. "Ben, you're going to wear a hole in my floors. Come and sit down."

"I can't. I don't know what to say to them."

"Don't try. Remember Paul? God will give you the words you need but you have to wait for the questions first."

He smiled then sat down beside her and took her hand. "I can't thank you enough. I couldn't do this alone."

"Well, I think you could but I'm glad to be here for moral support."

"You're more to me than moral support, Livvy."

Their eyes locked and the look of love in Ben's eyes stilled her breath. Memories engulfed her of being in his arms, of being held against his heart and losing herself in his kiss. Ben leaned closer. Her gaze went to his lips, and she started to close her eyes. They'd been dancing around this first kiss for weeks and she was ready to test the waters. She heard him whisper her name; her heart leaped into her throat with anticipation.

The moment shattered when the doorbell chimed.

She opened her eyes, trying to remember to breathe and regain her equilibrium.

Ben stood and Olivia gathered herself and went to the door. Ben followed behind. She opened the door to an attractive Asian couple with kind eyes.

"We're looking for Ben Kincaid."

Olivia smiled. "Please come in. We're expecting you."

Ben stepped forward and held out his hand. "Glad to meet you." He introduced Olivia.

They settled in the living room and Olivia offered drinks then took a seat in the far corner. Close enough in case Ben needed her, but far away enough so that they could converse privately.

Mr. Wong faced Ben. "We have questions. Many as a matter of fact and we're hoping you can answer them."

"I'll do my best, sir."

After a few moments, Olivia noticed Ben relax and took the opportunity to slip out of the room, offering up a prayer that this visit would ease some of Ben's guilt. He carried too much on his shoulders over their wedding and Davey's death. He needed to be absolved of that and it was time she did her part.

She'd realized after looking over her Good/ Bad list that somewhere along the line, she'd forgiven him for walking out. It still hurt, but she saw now that much of her pain was over being humiliated, dumped and having her perfect dream ruined. He'd done them both a favor because they were not ready to be married at that time. They both needed to grow up first.

Dottie had helped her realize that her priorities then had been backward. She should have been focused on their relationship, not the perfect font for the invitations.

Olivia tried to concentrate on her laptop, ostensibly working on the souvenir booklet, but it was useless. She'd stared at the screen and not made one change. Her thoughts were all in the other room with Ben.

She was aware of the hushed voices and once she thought she heard a soft cry. She couldn't imagine what Davey's mother must be feeling. It had been hard for Olivia to hear about Ben's ordeal. She'd cried herself to sleep afterward, curled into a fetal position, fighting waves of nausea as she thought about what he'd been through.

Her heart went out to the parents. Learning about what their son had endured would be more devastating. She sent off a prayer for them that they could draw a measure of comfort in what Ben was sharing.

Try as she might, she couldn't concentrate on anything as long as Davey's parents were here. She paced; she drank tea and doodled on a notepad. She wanted them to take all the time they needed, but she was also desperate to know how it was going.

Finally, the tone of the conversation changed and she heard soft mutterings as if they were saying goodbye. When she peeked into the living room she saw the couple walking out the front door.

She hurried to Ben's side and took his hand. There was a strange look on his face. "How did it go? What did they say?"

Ben smiled and slipped his arm around her waist. "Good. Very good. They didn't blame me at all. They thanked me for being his friend and for getting him to help after we were freed. Mostly they were happy that Davey had shown me the way to the Lord. They said it was his driving force, to share the Gospel with everyone."

"Did you tell them all of it?"

He nodded. "They wanted to know. I tried to spare them, but they weren't having it.

I told them everything and it hurt but they were so grateful. I don't think I'll look on that time the same way anymore. They were a great couple. I see now where Davey got his strength of character."

He hugged her. "Thank you for being here."

"I'm glad I could help."

He looked deeply into her eyes. "I always knew you had a caring heart, but I never realized how big it was until I came back. You are an amazing woman. The way you care for Charlie and everyone around you. You take my breath away, Livvy."

She touched his cheek. "When you first suggested that we take time to get to know each other, I thought it was pointless, but it made me look at you more closely and I was forced to reevaluate. I'm so proud of you. You're stronger than you think."

"Livvy, I wish we could…"

She knew what he was going to say. "I know. But we're friends now. Let's be content with that for the time being."

She tried to shut out the disappointment she saw in his eyes. She needed a little more time. She wasn't sure why, but the old hesitation lingered.

Chapter Ten

Olivia couldn't remember the last time she'd awakened in the morning feeling so excited about the day. Today was the two hundredth birthday of Blessing, Mississippi. This was the day she'd worked toward for three years. This celebration and the committee that created it had been her salvation. It had given her a reason to get up each morning, a job to conquer and goal to pursue. It had changed her from a quiet, insecure accountant into a woman in charge of her life and possibly the next town manager.

But today was all about having fun and enjoying the fruits of her hard work. She had a few responsibilities today, but most of the day's events would be handled by other committee chairs, leaving her free to be a regular citizen and enjoy the festivities.

Mostly she wanted to share all the fun with Charlie. Exposing him to new adventures and new places had become her favorite pastime. She'd show him the whole world if she could. But for now, she'd be content to show him the wonders of her small hometown.

After making her way to the kitchen, she filled her favorite cup with coffee and took it outside on the porch. The weather was getting warmer every day. Soon, the perfect balmy days of May would take over, and she couldn't wait.

She'd nearly emptied her cup when the door opened and Charlie and Rudy burst onto the porch.

"Is today the birthday party? Can I have cake for breakfast?"

Olivia laughed and pulled him into her lap. "No. It's not that kind of birthday, but we'll have a lot of fun today and there'll be lots of yummy food to eat. There'll be games and a parade, and a big picnic, and tonight there'll be fireworks."

"What's that?"

She chuckled then used her hands to demonstrate. "That's where they shoot rockets into the sky and they explode into pretty colors."

"Can Rudy come with us to the party today?"

"No. Dogs aren't allowed."

He stuck out his lower lip. "But he'll be lonely without us."

Olivia thought a moment. How like her nephew to think of others. "Well, what if we ask Miss Nora to watch him while we're gone? He likes it at her house."

Charlie smiled and snuggled closer. "'Kay."

Oh, how she loved this little boy. Everything he said or did fascinated her. She couldn't imagine her life without him.

"When can we go?"

"Not for a while yet. You have to have breakfast, then get dressed. We'll go as soon as Ben gets here."

Charlie scrambled off her lap and ran to the door. "I want breakfast now."

She could see there would be no tempering her nephew's excitement today. Her only hope was to keep him busy until Ben arrived. He'd had photos to take of the mayor's formal speech and comments and recognition from committee members and other local businessmen. Then the official opening of the day. After that, Ben was free to spend the day with her and Charlie. There were more than enough camerapeople to cover everything. Journalists from all over the state would be here, along with local papers and other media.

By the time Ben showed up, Olivia was

nearing exhaustion. He stepped inside and gave her a worried look. "Are you okay?"

"I'm not sure. Try keeping a four year old occupied for an hour when all he wants to do is go to the big party."

Ben laughed and called to the boy. "Hey, little buddy, are you ready to celebrate the town's birthday?"

He ran to Ben. "We have to leave Rudy at Miss Nora's. Dogs can't go."

"Can little boys go?" Charlie nodded vigorously. "Then let's get going."

They started their day at the children's area, where Charlie had a puppy painted on his cheek. They watched the parade of historic moments in Blessing history and a long line of first responder vehicles from around the county. Charlie was impressed with the hook-and-ladder trucks from the fire department. Ben promised to get him a toy one.

It was so easy to spoil the little guy and Olivia enjoyed every moment of it.

The morning flew by and Charlie started to proclaim his hunger. They walked to the Riverbank Park and purchased a picnic lunch, then settled at a table beneath an old live oak tree.

They'd nearly finished when Ben suddenly stiffened and stared into the distance.

"Something wrong?"

"I don't know." He raised his hand and waved at someone. "My brother Jeff is here."

She followed Ben's gaze and saw a tall dark-haired man with a neat beard coming toward them. "Why do you suppose he's here?"

Ben shook his head then stood and greeted his older brother. "What brings you to this neck of the woods?"

"You."

Ben cleared his throat. "Jeff, this is Olivia Marshall and her nephew, Charlie. Livvy, this is my brother Jeff."

They exchanged pleasantries but it was obvious to Olivia that they wanted to speak privately. "Charlie wants to ride the little train around the square. I'll catch up with you later. Nice to have met you, Jeff."

She took Charlie's hand and walked toward the path, resisting the urge to turn around and look at the brothers. She took comfort from knowing that this brother was the one who had cared for Ben when he'd come home.

If only she could be in two places at once. Riding the train with Charlie and sitting beside Ben in case he needed her.

Ben waited until Livvy was out of earshot then glared at his brother. "What brings you here?"

"Don't I even get a *hi, how are you* or *glad to see you*?"

Ben rubbed his temple. He owed his brother better. "Sorry. You know I'm always glad to see you, but you didn't give me a warning. That's not like you."

"I know, but this came up suddenly and I wanted to strategize in person."

Ben's chest tightened. Something was really wrong. "About what?" Jeff took a deep breath as if readying himself to deliver bad news. Ben braced.

"Mom got it into her head that you've been brainwashed, and she's decided to do something about it."

"Like what?"

"She's convinced Dad that you're part of some religious cult and she's determined to rescue you."

Ben would have laughed if he wasn't so angry. "Christianity isn't a cult."

Jeff nodded. "I know. I understand completely but Mom wants Dad to hire a deprogrammer to fix you and bring you back in the fold."

"You're not serious?"

Jeff pinned him with a steady gaze, spiking Ben's anger. "Why can't they accept that I've found my faith and leave it at that?"

"I don't know. But I know Dad is looking at hiring someone and these people are known to use physical means if necessary. Like kidnapping?"

"They're going to kidnap me, and talk me out of believing in God? How would that work exactly?"

"I just want you to be on your guard for any suspicious guys lurking around, that's all. I've tried explaining things to them but they don't get it." Jeff held his gaze a long moment. "How are you, really?"

"Good. Really good. Coming here was the right thing to do."

"You look happy. Better than I've seen you in a long time. I take it that has something to do with Olivia and the boy?"

"Yeah. They're very important to me. I care for them both a great deal. They've changed my life."

"Does that mean things between you and her are all patched up?"

It was a complicated question and Ben took his time forming a reply. "Not completely. Things are better. We've learned to work together and we've become friends in a way we never were back then. Livvy has forgiven me for walking out on our wedding, but I don't think she'll ever fully trust me again."

"Is that what you want?"

He didn't hesitate. "Yes. If I could I'd reschedule the wedding for tomorrow."

"Have you told her about your future plans?"

He should have expected this question. "No. Not yet."

"Why not? If things have progressed this far, shouldn't she know you want to go into the ministry? Don't you start classes next month?"

Ben wished he could skip over this topic. "Yes, but there's plenty of time."

"Hey, this is me you're talking to. I know this is hard but you've got to tell her at some point, and it seems to me that the longer you put it off the worse her reaction."

Surely his brother understood his reluctance. "Worse than my parents disowning me when I told them I'd accepted faith in Jesus and was going to become a minister." A sardonic laughed escaped his lips. "Or having the woman I cared about turn her back when I told her because she didn't want to be poor forever."

"Do you really expect Olivia to react the same way?"

Ben shook his head. "No. But there's been so much between us and there's more to unravel. I'm gun-shy I guess."

Jeff laid his hand on Ben's arm. "I'm just trying to look out for you. I'm afraid of what might happen the first time something goes really wrong. Something so big it rocks your core, and then you'll find yourself back in that black hole. I don't want to see that happen. Maybe you should come home with me. We'll deal with the folks together."

Ben set his jaw. Did his brother really think he was that fragile that the first setback would break him again? "Now you have no faith in me?"

"It's not faith. It's about progress. I remember where you were when you came home from Europe, how you wouldn't talk to anyone or see anyone but me for months. I don't want to see that happen again."

"I know. It won't. I'm stronger now. I'm not that person. As far as the guilt goes, Livvy and I have worked that out, and meeting with Davey's parents eased that situation. I know the memories will always be there and they'll probably sneak up on me now and again, but I've got my trusty tools, my candy and the scripture. I'll be fine. I can't image anything that could be so bad that it would knock me off-kilter again."

Jeff shrugged. "Okay. I'll leave it to you but remember what I said about Dad. Be on guard. And please tell Livvy what you're planning to do. If she does turn away, best do it now before things get any more complicated."

Ben knew he was right, but his hesitance lingered. He'd find the right time soon. But not today. Today was a fun day with the two people he loved most, and he wasn't going to let anything dampen their spirits.

After saying goodbye to his brother, Ben went in search of Livvy and Charlie. On the way he passed a prize booth and filled out a card for a possibility to win a child's motorized truck, something he knew Charlie would love. The booth attendant took the card and glanced at it, then at Ben. His expression darkened and his lips pressed into a hard line.

"Ben Kincaid, is it? I thought you looked familiar. You're the guy who walked out on Olivia. Left her in that church alone and brokenhearted."

Ben blinked in surprise, totally unprepared for the verbal assault. "Yes, sir. I am." His pulse raced as his memory of that day rushed into his mind along with the huge load of regret.

"You should be ashamed of yourself. Better yet, run out of town. What are you doing here?"

"I'm working with Olivia on the bicentennial committee."

The man snorted. "What are you trying to do, rub salt in her wounds?"

"No, sir. We've made our peace."

The man crossed his arms over his chest. "You had better not hurt that sweet girl. What you did was cowardly."

"Yes, sir. It was. And I'll regret it until the day I die."

The man's expression softened a bit. "You threw away something special, young man. I hope you realize that."

Ben's throat contracted. He could barely squeeze out the words. "I do." He turned and walked away, struck by the irony of those words. He should have said *I do* when it mattered most.

Ben tracked Olivia and Charlie down at the petting zoo. One look at Livvy and he knew she had a truckload of questions, but he'd share his visit with Jeff later. Right now he wanted to enjoy being with his little family.

A family he prayed could be his one day. God willing.

Olivia turned off the kitchen light and returned to the living room that evening, her heart filled to overflowing with joy. It had been a perfect day. All the bicentennial events had gone off without a hitch; the crowds were huge, the speeches short and the fireworks at the end of the day spectacular. The committee and all the volunteers had done themselves proud.

She sat on the sofa smiling at Ben and Charlie in the comfy chair. Exhausted after his bath, the little guy had crawled up into Ben's lap and fallen asleep, and Ben showed no signs of carrying him to his bed.

He smiled over at her and her heart melted. It did that a lot when she saw her two guys together. "I think we wore him out."

"No doubt. But I think he had a great time. I did." He glanced at her and his eyes held that look of affection she remembered so well. She'd started to see it a lot but she couldn't quite trust that it was real. They'd become friends, something she'd doubted would ever happen. Working with him, learning about his past and seeing how much he'd changed had brought her heart closer to falling for him again. Very close.

Ben finally shifted in the chair and scooped Charlie up and carried him down to his room. Olivia allowed herself a moment to imagine this was the way every night would be. Her and Ben, watching over Charlie as he grew, taking him on adventures and fun trips.

Ben returned and sat beside her on the sofa. "Did you have a good day?"

"Of course. It was perfect in every way."

"Good. I like to see you happy."

"I haven't had a chance to ask you about Jeff. What did he want?" She saw Ben stiffen slightly. "Is everything okay?"

"It will be. He wanted to tell me that my parents think I've been brainwashed into a cult."

"I don't understand."

"They were not happy when I became a believer. They think I've turned my back on what they consider right. My mom is convinced that I need to be deprogramed out of my faith."

"That's ridiculous. Faith in Jesus isn't a cult."

"I know. Jeff wanted to warn me in person that they might be looking to hire someone to try and deprogram me, and he wanted to make sure I was doing all right."

"He sounds like a good brother."

"He is. I couldn't have made it through coming home without him." He shifted and took her hand. "Livvy, there are still things I need to tell you. Things I want to explain about my future, but not tonight."

"Is it serious?"

He nodded. "Possibly life-changing."

"Now you have me worried."

"No, it's nothing like that. I promise we'll talk soon." He kissed her cheek then stood. "It's late. I'll see you tomorrow."

She walked him to the door. "It was a wonderful day. Thank you."

He placed his hand on the side of her neck. "Thank you. Today was the first time in a long time that I felt completely normal."

She smiled. "No shadows?"

"Not a one."

His thumb gently stroked her cheek and she leaned into him and waited. But the kiss didn't come. He held her gaze a long moment then turned and left. She watched him cross the street, wishing she had made the first move. Why hadn't she?

Chapter Eleven

Olivia fastened Charlie's shoes then stood back and surveyed her little guy. "You look so handsome."

Charlie smoothed his shirt and looked up at her. "Do I look like Big Ben?"

She chuckled and gave him a hug. "You look exactly like Big Ben." He grinned and dashed off to show Rudy his new outfit.

They'd gone shopping this morning for new clothes. He'd been in dire need of everything, since the things he'd had with him were either wearing out or getting too small. She'd had so much fun in the children's department. Charlie liked everything, until he spotted a shirt like the ones Ben favored. The casual knit Henley style with the buttons near the throat. From that moment on, he only wanted to find clothes that were like Big Ben's. They found little jeans, boots, a jacket and even a button-up cotton shirt for church; all were as close to Ben's outfits as they could find.

Now the little fellow was bubbling over with anticipation to show his hero that they matched. Olivia had to admit, she was eager to see them side by side and she knew Ben would be so pleased and flattered that Charlie wanted to dress like him.

Unfortunately, Ben wouldn't be here until later in the evening. He had a group meeting to attend but once he was home they were going to finalize a surprise for Charlie. With the bicentennial over and time on their hands, they were planning a trip for Charlie to the beach on the weekend. She couldn't wait to introduce him to the sand and the waves and water.

Her booklet had been sent to the printers with compliments from Delores. The committee would disband soon and the members would either go back to their regular jobs or find new ones. She'd filled out the application for the town manager position and the powers that be had assured her she had the inside track. Now it sat in an email waiting to be sent. For some reason she couldn't bring herself to submit it and she didn't know why.

She looked at Charlie and smiled. It was

probably because she was having too much fun being with Charlie to think about work.

Charlie sat up and made a face. "I'm hungry."

"Me too. What should we have for supper?"

"Will Big Ben be here?"

"No. Remember he is eating with his friends at church tonight, but he'll be here later." Charlie's bottom lip poked out. He missed Ben every minute when he was gone. "How about we order pizza? We haven't had any in a while."

Charlie nodded, a big smile on his face. "Rudy likes it too."

She ruffled his hair then reached for her phone. "I'm sure he does but he'll have to settle for dog food."

Charlie looked the dog in the face. "Sorry, Rudy. Mommy says no pizza for you."

Olivia caught her breath. He'd never called her that before. She probably should correct him, but what would it hurt? Besides, she liked the soft gooey sensation around her heart. She decided to ignore it for now.

The pizza arrived and they'd barely taken a bite when someone pounded on the front door.

"Olivia."

Her heart dropped into her stomach. Loretta. She opened the door and her sister pushed right in. "What are you doing here? You're supposed to be in St. Thomas."

Loretta looked around. "That didn't work out. Where's Charlie?"

The little boy stood in the kitchen arch peeking around the corner. She saw him and grabbed his arm. "Thanks for watching him. I have to run. I've got to meet someone."

"What? Who? You can't take him now. It's almost bedtime." Charlie was pulling against his mother, trying to get free.

"He can sleep in the car. It's a long drive to Nashville."

"Nashville? What happened to the rich guy on the island?"

"It fizzled out. But this new guy is the real thing. He's a family man. He and Charlie will get along great."

Olivia's mind spun. "No, Loretta, you can't just waltz in here and take him." Olivia took Charlie's other arm and tried to pull him close but her sister wouldn't let go.

Her sister scowled. "Oh? I'm his mother. I can do what I like."

Olivia's fear swelled. "But he's happy here. He has a dog. People who love him."

"He'll be happy there too." She started toward the door.

Charlie started to cry. "No. I want to stay with Aunt 'Livia and Big Ben."

"Well, you can't. Come on."

Olivia grabbed her arm. "What about his things? I need time to pack and find Rudy's leash and…"

"Oh, no. No animals are coming with me. I'll get what he needs when we arrive." She opened the door.

"Loretta, you can't do this." Desperation took over. She had to find a way to stop her sister.

"But I am."

Charlie had started to cry harder. "Aunt 'Livia. I don't want to go."

She reached out and took his little arm. "Loretta, let me say goodbye."

"No time." She opened the door and Charlie leaned out of his mother's arms, reaching for her. "I don't want to go. I want to stay here."

"Be quiet!"

As she crossed the porch Charlie started to scream. "No. I want to stay. I want Aunt 'Livia and Big Ben and Rudy."

"You're coming with me."

"Nooooo!" Charlie squirmed and kicked in

his mother's arms and reached out for help, his face wet with tears.

"Loretta, for the love of God, listen to him. He doesn't want to go. Please leave him here." Her heart was breaking. She didn't realize she was crying until she felt wetness on her face.

Charlie was kicking harder now, trying to pull out of his mother's grasp. Olivia was afraid she'd drop him. She ran behind her sister, trying to reach her nephew. Loretta shoved him in the car and turned to face her.

Olivia grabbed her arm. "Can't you see he's afraid? Think of what you're doing to him. He's just a baby."

"He'll be fine. He's going to be the family my friend wants."

"What does that mean?"

Loretta slid into the car and slammed the door. The last thing Olivia heard was Charlie crying for his truck. Her spirit died as the car pulled away. Her first thought was to call Ben, but her mind was so tormented all she could manage was to text the word *help*.

The car disappeared down the street. Something cold touched her fingers and she glanced down to see Rudy looking up at her. Tears broke free; her heart shriveled into a dark knot in her chest.

Somehow she made her way to the porch

and sat down, drained of all strength and emotion. This must be what it felt like to be dead. She couldn't think, couldn't feel; she was an empty shell devoid of hope and life.

Her whole being ached to hold the frightened little boy in her arms and make him feel safe. What would her sister do with him? He'd be hungry. He'd hardly eaten, and how would he go to sleep without Rudy at his feet? And Ben, Charlie didn't have a chance to say goodbye to Ben or to Nora.

Fear for her nephew grew, filling her mind with terrifying possibilities. Would he withdraw again? He must be so scared. She didn't trust her sister to care for him properly. Not the way she and Ben could.

She glanced up, her gaze taking in the neighborhood. There were houses clustered close together, their lights shining from their windows. Still, she felt alone and desolate.

She'd only felt this way one other time.

On her wedding day.

Maybe it was time to accept that she was supposed to spend her life alone.

So very, very alone.

Ben hurried up the porch steps and found Olivia sitting in the wicker chair staring into the distance. She didn't look at him or move.

For a second, he wasn't sure she was even breathing.

"Olivia." He approached her gradually, before stooping down and lightly touching her arm. Slowly, she turned her gaze to meet his. The raw pain in her eyes frightened him. All he knew was that Livvy had texted him with one word. *Help.* Thankfully he'd been on his way home from church and only minutes from the house. His mind had imagined all kinds of scenarios. But Olivia looked unharmed except for the pain in her eyes, which told a different story.

"What happened?"

It took her a moment to respond. "He's gone."

"Who?"

"Charlie. She took him. I couldn't stop her." She looked him in the eyes. "I needed you. I needed help but you weren't here." She stood, her gaze turned dark and angry. "You're never here when you're supposed to be. You weren't there for the wedding and you weren't here for Charlie."

"I was at church for my group and family night supper, remember?"

She shook her head. "I remember. You just disappear without a word. A no-show."

A strangled laugh escaped her throat. "Nora's no-show nephew."

She gasped and put her hands over her face. "Oh, Ben. I'm sorry. I didn't mean that—you know I didn't."

Ben knew she was distraught and not thinking clearly but the accusation still stung.

She grabbed her stomach and bent over. "Oh, God, please help me."

She started to collapse, and Ben caught her and led her back to the chair. "Livvy. I don't understand. Who took Charlie? Where is he?"

"Loretta. She just showed up and she took him, and he was screaming for me but she wouldn't listen. She put him in the car and drove away."

"Why did she take him?"

"A new guy. A rich guy. Something about making a family."

"Do you know where she went? I'll try and catch her? Did she say where she was going?"

"Nashville." Olivia shook her head. "She was so cold. Charlie was reaching for me, yelling for Rudy, but she ignored him and put him in the car. I couldn't do anything to stop her."

Ben's heart and mind were churning in a hurricane of conflicting emotions. He was worried for Olivia, angry at her sister and terrified for little Charlie. Mostly he felt helpless to do anything about any of it.

"Did you call the police?"

Olivia nodded. "They said unless I feared for his life, his mother had every right to come and pick him up from a babysitter." Her hands clutched the front of her blouse. "I'm more than a babysitter."

The wind had picked up and rain was coming down, blowing onto the porch. "Come on, Livvy, let's go inside." He settled her on the sofa. She moved as if she was in a trance. He sat beside her, but she wouldn't look at him or speak. Rudy came up and laid his chin on her knee. She shivered and burst into heart-wrenching sobs.

"Oh, Ben, that baby was so scared. He didn't want to go. He was begging me to help him, and I couldn't do anything. I pleaded with Loretta. I didn't know she could be so cruel."

The realization of what had happened started to sink in, twisting his gut and pressing on his lungs like a two-ton weight.

"Oh, Ben." Livvy leaned into his arms, clutching his shirt in her fist and crying so hard he was worried she might pass out.

"He's so little. What will happen to him? What if she doesn't take care of him? He's going to be so scared and alone. I should have been able to keep him. He needed me and I let him down. What if the guy she's meeting treats him badly? He doesn't even have his favorite truck. I tried to get Loretta to take Rudy, but it only made her madder. I'm so worried. He's so little. He's just a baby."

Ben held her close, his own heart shredded at the loss and burning with worry for the child he'd come to love.

An hour later, he closed the door to Olivia's bedroom and made his way quietly to the kitchen. He'd promised her he'd stay in the house tonight. She didn't want to be alone. After fixing a drink and sandwich he sat at the table to eat, only to discover the thought of food made his stomach churn.

He lowered his head into his hands and prayed for Charlie. For his safety, for his comfort. If only he could have taken his beloved truck. Loretta's care of her son was in question. Charlie had come to them neglected and withdrawn but over his time here, thanks to Livvy and his Aunt Nora, he'd become a happy, funny, energetic little guy.

He groaned. Being with his mother could wipe out all his growth. What kind of life would he have from here on?

In a rash moment earlier, and needing des-

perately to give Olivia hope, he'd promised
to track her sister down and find a way to
get Charlie back. Now he was regretting that
promise. He wasn't a lawyer but he doubted if
an aunt held any sway over the child's mother.

Exhausted, he stretched out on the sofa.
Rudy joined him and they fell asleep, but
Ben's rest was interrupted frequently by bad
dreams and the old nightmare. He woke with
a shout then froze waiting to see if he'd awakened Olivia. Convinced she was still sleeping, he unwrapped a candy, turned the TV
on, muted the sound and let the twenty-four-
hour sports network play. It did little to dis-
tract him.

His gaze fell on Charlie's toys stored in
the corner and his heart broke. "Oh, my little
buddy." Tears rolled down his cheeks. There
was a huge hole in his life now. One he had
no idea how to fill, and no idea on how to fix
this mess for Olivia.

The old guilt churned to life. He'd come
here to face his guilt and deal with it. But
now he had a new layer to battle. He wasn't
sure he had the strength.

He had to find a way to rescue that little
boy, but he feared there was no solution. Olivia was his aunt, not his mother, and her
claims to his custody were paper-thin.

Finally he broke down and called Nora for help, knowing he would probably wake her but needing to connect with someone. She broke down in tears when he told her what had happened.

"I wish I'd been here—maybe I could have helped somehow. Poor Olivia having to deal with that all alone. I can't imagine what she was going through."

Ben's conscience stung. He should have been there for her. His logical mind told him he'd had no idea that Loretta would suddenly appear and take Charlie away, but he still felt as if he'd failed Olivia. "I'm worried about her. I've never seen her like this. It's as if she stopped existing."

"In a way she has. That little boy had become her life. She's lost. She needs you more than ever now."

"But I can't do anything to help. I don't even know where to start. I feel empty and useless." He heard rustling on the other end of the call.

"I know where you can start. With a call to George Freeman. He's a local attorney who specializes in family law. If nothing else, he can tell you where to go from here. I'll send you his number."

Ben left Freeman's office the next morning irritated and frustrated. He'd convinced Livvy to stay home. He didn't want to get her hopes up for nothing. Sadly, the attorney had little positive to say. As Charlie's aunt, her chances of gaining custody of her nephew were slim. Olivia's only option was to prove her sister an unfit mother, which Ben had serious doubts of accomplishing. While Loretta wasn't the best mother on the planet, there was no proof that she had physically abused the child or left him alone at any time.

He went back to Olivia's with a knot in his stomach and a pressure in his chest that made breathing a chore. She opened the door and his disappointment must have been written on his face because he saw hope dawn and instantly fade in her eyes.

She turned away, wiping her tears. Rudy trotted at her side and curled up at her feet when she sat on the sofa. "There's no hope, is there? We've lost him forever."

Ben sat beside her and pulled her close. "I'm not giving up. But Mr. Freeman confirmed what I suspected. The only way you can petition for custody is if you can prove Loretta is an unfit mother. Is there anything that happened that might help us?"

She shook her head. "I don't think so. Charlie was lacking love and attention but I doubt that would win a custody charge."

Ben's heart ripped in two at the despair in her voice. He had to do something. He had to find a way to fix this not only for Olivia, but for Charlie and, selfishly, for himself. He didn't know how long he could endure not knowing how his little buddy was.

Olivia rested her head against his shoulder and he kissed her forehead. "I promise you I'll fix this, Livvy. I don't know how but I won't stop until that little boy is back here where he belongs."

"What are you going to do?"

"I have no idea. But I know where I'm going to start."

He began to formulate a plan the moment he walked out of Olivia's house. Back at Nora's, his first call was to Jeff to run his idea by him. His brother didn't think it would work but he encouraged him to try.

Steeling himself, Ben dialed his father's number, his last words to him ricocheting through his mind. *"Don't come to me for help."* Ben's blood chilled when he heard his father's voice, but he set his jaw and made his request. All that mattered now was getting Charlie back. He'd endure anything to make that happen.

Nora watched him closely when he came into the kitchen. "Well. What did he say?"

Ben sat at the table, drained and yet hopeful. "A lot. The bulk of it directed at my foolish life choices. I agreed with everything he said except for coming back home." He held up his phone. "But he did agree to give me the number of his high-powered lawyer. He's bailed my dad out of several complicated messes. Maybe he'll have some legal trick that'll help us with Charlie."

"Have you called him?"

"He's not available until tomorrow. I'm going to head down to New Orleans and be in his office first thing in the morning."

"Are you taking Olivia with you?"

"No. I don't want her there if it all falls through. I'd better tackle this alone. Will you check in on her while I'm gone?"

"Of course. But I think you should tell her."

Ben shook his head. "I can't give her any more bad news. I'm not going to do anything until I can tell her Charlie is coming home."

"What if you can't make that happen?"

Ben shut down the negative comment. "I have to. I can't fail her again."

Olivia stood outside the door to Charlie's room and told herself to walk away and try to forget, but the memories she'd collected of her nephew were there, replaying in her mind every moment. She understood Ben's struggle with his captivity better now. Something so devastating couldn't simply be brushed aside. It was like a canker sore that ate away at you, always painful, always reminding you it was there.

Every breath she drew held pinpricks of pain. It was all she could do to get through the day. Somehow, she reported for work to complete final details and start clearing out her things. Her job was over. The committee would disband over the next few weeks and she had no idea what she would do now.

Ben had stopped by briefly to tell her he was going to New Orleans to meet with an attorney who might be able to help them with Charlie. He'd acted so strangely, so distant and remote that she suspected he wasn't planning on returning. She couldn't blame him. If she could run away somewhere, she would.

Marcy Jo entered her office and stopped at her desk. "You look awful."

"Thank you. I'm glad to know I look as bad on the outside as I feel inside."

Marcy Jo sat down. "I didn't mean it that way. I know you're hurting. I wish I could do something for you. And Ben. Where is he?"

"Gone."

"What do you mean?"

"He's gone to New Orleans to see a big-shot lawyer. He thinks he can help."

"That's encouraging. When will he be back?"

Olivia set her jaw and faced her friend. "Let's not kid ourselves. Ben isn't coming back."

"You don't know that."

"I do. This is different. The pain of losing Charlie has crushed both of us. Ben loves that little boy. He's hurting as much as I am. More, maybe." She'd started to worry that this might drag him back down into his PTSD black hole. Maybe it was best that he'd left town. He didn't need to be exposed to the memories here.

"Then I would think he'd try harder to make things right." Marcy Jo crossed her arms over her chest. "That man loves you."

Olivia appreciated what her friend was trying to do but it was pointless. "No. I see now that the only thing holding us together was our shared love for Charlie."

Marcy Jo made a disgusted sound. "I don't believe that, but you're right, this is different. This time it's real. This time it's not all fun and games—you two were a team, a great team. Not only with Charlie but on this project. Did you know that someone called here and asked about hiring Ben? He's gaining a reputation as a skilled photographer."

She was happy for him. It was obvious he enjoyed working with his camera. "That's good. Did he take it?"

"No."

Olivia nodded, her throat closing. "Because he knew he was leaving. It's what he does."

Marcy Jo glared and set her hands on her hips. "You need to stop making that assumption every time he leaves the room. He might come back and have great news about getting the little guy back."

Olivia ignored her friend.

Marcy Jo came closer and rested her hands on the desktop. "Girl, I know you love him. You've fallen for him again, only you're too scared to believe it's real. You've still got it in your head that he's going to vanish one day like he did before. I get it. He hurt you deeply, but that's not the man I see today. Can you honestly say he's not a completely different guy?"

Olivia stared at her hands. She couldn't. But right now, her emotions were so knotted up, she couldn't think clearly either. Her heart ached for Charlie, but it also ached for Ben in different ways. Somehow, he'd claimed her heart again but she was still holding on to it, afraid to let it slip from her grasp for fear of being hurt again, and she had no idea how to change that.

Marcy Jo straightened. "Olivia, I've known you a long time and I love you like a sister, but I think you have deeper issues than trusting Ben. You're holding up trust like it's the only quality that matters. I'm glad the Good Lord doesn't hold us to that kind of impossible level. He doesn't withhold His affections when we mess up. Maybe you should make a list for yourself and write down all the reasons you're still holding a grudge."

Olivia bristled. "It's not a grudge."

Marcy Jo scowled. "Isn't it?"

Olivia dismissed her friend's observation. Marcy Jo didn't understand. To her dismay and irritation, however, her comment refused to leave her thoughts and each time it scraped a deeper furrow in her mind until she left the office and headed for the Blessing Bridge.

She crossed the arched landmark and made her way to the small Greek-style garden folly. It was secluded and quiet and she needed both. The stone bench was cool and faced the lovely arched bridge that at this time of year had a garland of wisteria along the railing.

A grudge. Ridiculous. She didn't carry grudges. She closed her eyes and sat quietly, waiting. A word formed in her mind.

Resentment.

The definition flowed through her mind and into her conscience with burning sensation. She pressed her hand against her mouth as the truth hit home. She was harboring resentment toward Ben. What an ugly realization about herself. A sob clogged her throat. *"Oh, Lord, forgive me. I didn't know. I didn't realize."*

She had been holding a grudge against Ben. Perhaps, subconsciously, she wanted to hurt him as much as he'd hurt her. But not anymore. Marcy Jo was right. It was time to do some serious soul-searching. She wiped her tears and headed back to her car. But it would have to wait.

Until she knew how Charlie was, she couldn't consider anything else. Especially her feelings for Ben. In the meantime, she had no choice but to move forward. She just didn't know how to do that.

Olivia woke the next morning reluctant to get out of bed and face the day. Without Charlie, her entire world was pointless. She walked to the front window and looked outside. Even the colorful bushes that always lifted her spirits looked faded and uninspiring. All she knew was that she was completely alone. That was the one thing she hadn't acknowledged back then. Despite all her accomplishments and her growth, she was still alone. Her bungalow was charming, perfectly decorated, but she came back to it each day by herself.

Then Ben had reappeared and invaded her life, and Charlie had come to stay, and she'd fought her way through resentment and hurt and fear and found a different person inside. One who wanted a family, who wanted things she'd never considered before. Ben had shown her that she could still fall in love with him. Charlie had exposed a love so deep and tender it was frightening at times.

All that was gone again. Charlie was with Loretta, Ben was gone on a wild-goose chase and she didn't even have the bicentennial job to take up her time.

Her life was little more than a leaf in the wind with no direction, no purpose, simply drifting on the breeze. Utterly lost. She wasn't who she used to be and not who she'd become.

She walked back to her sofa and sat down, staring at her laptop. The application for the town manager job filled the screen. It was not what she wanted, but she needed to pay the bills. She moved her cursor to the send button and paused. A car was pulling up out front. Ben?

She hurried to the door; a little boy was running up the sidewalk and onto... She opened the door just in time to catch Charlie as he threw himself at her. He wrapped his arms around her neck and she held him tightly to her chest.

"I missed you, Aunt 'Livia."

Tears stung her eyes and her throat convulsed. "I missed you so much, sweetie." Rudy was jumping up and down welcoming his little owner back. Charlie giggled and patted Olivia's cheeks, bringing a fresh set of tears. He wrapped his arms around her neck again and clung to her fiercely.

"Rudy missed me too."

Olivia wiped her cheeks.

"You were always so emotional." Loretta stepped into the room and shut the door.

"What are you doing here?"

"I'm bringing him back. He's whined the whole time for you and that dog."

Olivia steered her to the kitchen. Charlie had run down the hall to his room. "What's going on? Charlie's not a dog you can park at a kennel whenever he's inconvenient."

She shrugged. "He'll be here a while."

"What happened?"

"The guy didn't want any old kid. He wanted one of his own and I said no way. I'm not going to go through that again."

"Olivia."

The sound of Ben's deep voice sent a rush of relief through her system. All her resentment and irritation vanished.

"In here."

"Big Ben." Charlie heard him too and raced toward him, nearly climbing up his legs to be held.

Ben was speechless. He held the little boy close, his hand cradling the small head. His eyes were closed, and Olivia's heart tugged. There could be no doubt that he loved Charlie as much as she did and he'd suffered his loss as deeply.

"I'm glad you're back, little buddy."

"Rudy's glad too. He jumped on me and knocked me down. I'm okay though. It didn't hurt."

"Good to know. I don't want you to be hurt." He looked at Loretta. "By anyone, at any time."

She rolled her eyes. "Now that we're all caught up, I'll leave." She grabbed up her purse and started for the door.

In one smooth motion, Ben set Charlie on the floor then moved to the front door and stood in front of it like a palace guard. Olivia held her breath. She had no idea what he intended to do.

"We need to have a talk."

"No, we don't." She tried to move past but Ben held his ground.

"Sit down." Loretta raised her chin defiantly but Ben squared his shoulders and glared. "I can help you with that if you'd like."

The deep, hard tone of his voice sent a chill through Olivia. She'd never seen him like this. She'd have to add another entry to her list. Fierce defender.

Loretta fumed but finally sat in the armchair. "What do you want?"

"Charlie."

"What are you talking about?"

"I, that is, Olivia and I have been talking and we think it's best for Charlie's sake to have a stable home here with her. She wants custody of her nephew. Legal custody."

Loretta scoffed. "Not likely."

Olivia's determination rose from the gray muck she'd lost it in. "It is likely, Loretta. I want to be his legal guardian. It would be best if you signed away your rights to him completely." She sensed Ben staring at her.

He might have thrown her a curve with his suggestion, but she was going to embrace it and fight for her nephew.

"So, you have your little family and now you want me to just disappear—is that it?"

"No. It's true we love Charlie. He's happy here, Loretta. You saw him the day you took him away. He was hysterical. He's just a baby. He needs security. We… I can give him that. You can't. Not with your…unpredictable lifestyle."

Loretta leaned back in the chair; Olivia could see she was weighing her options. "What's in it for me?"

"Freedom. You can come and go as you like, follow any whim, chase whatever rainbow catches your eye."

She stood. "I'll think about it."

Ben resumed his place in front of the door. "We want it all legal. No loopholes."

"Fine." She reached for the doorknob.

Ben clamped down on her forearm. "You won't leave town until it's all signed, legal and aboveboard."

"How are you going to stop me?"

Olivia came forward and touched her sister's shoulder. "Please, Loretta. For once think of little Charlie and think of the freedom you'll have. You both win."

"Fine." She glared at Ben, who stepped aside. She opened the door. "But don't drag this thing out. It had better happen fast. I don't want to waste any time."

"I'll call you as soon as it's done. Leave me a number where I can reach you. Where will you be staying?"

She grinned. "With a friend."

Ben pulled out his phone and tapped in the number she gave him.

"Can I go now?"

"Thank you, Loretta. It's best for everyone."

"Whatever."

Olivia watched her sister stride away and get into her car. Her heart ached. Her sister had no idea what she was losing. She'd always been selfish and self-centered, but Olivia never dreamed she'd give up her only child.

Her heart and mind were pulled in two directions. Her heart was grateful that Charlie would be safe with her from now on, but she'd never understand how a mother could so blithely hand over her child in exchange for freedom and no responsibility.

Tears trailed down her cheeks. Ben came up behind her and took her shoulders in his hands. "Are you going to be all right?"

She nodded. "I will be now." She turned and faced him. "What made you think of the guardianship?"

"A long conversation with my dad's attorney. He couldn't help, but he suggested you do anything you could to gain custody." He wiped a tear from her cheek. "It seemed to me that if you didn't have some sort of legal claim to Charlie, your sister could come and go and treat you like a servant. That wouldn't be good for you or our little buddy."

She slid her arms around his waist, resting her head against his chest. "Thank you. I couldn't have made it through this without you. I'm glad you came back."

"Did you think I wouldn't?"

She searched for an answer. Admitting the truth would tell him she still didn't trust him and that wasn't completely true. "It crossed my mind."

He held her a little closer. "I'm sorry, Livvy. I promise I won't disappear again. If I have to leave, I'll tell you. I'll give you notice."

She pulled back and looked him in the eyes. The blue depths were clear and unclouded. "Promise?"

He nodded, brushing a strand of hair from her forehead. "I won't ever hurt you like that again. I know it's hard for you to believe, but I'll keep trying until you trust me again."

He looked deeply into her eyes, releasing the last piece of shielding in her heart.

"All I ever wanted was for you to be happy, Livvy."

She reached up and touched his cheek. He leaned forward, his lips a breath away. He said her name softly and she met his kiss. Her mind swirled with memories old and new and the sensation of being safe in his arms.

She relived the kiss long after he'd left, and she drifted to sleep filled with joy and contentment. Her boys were back, safe and permanent.

The Lord had blessed her greatly.

Chapter Twelve

Olivia took her seat at the conference table, her gaze trained on the empty chair across from her. Would Loretta show up? Would she actually sign the papers giving up her parental rights to her son?

Relinquishing her claim to her own flesh and blood was a situation Olivia could never imagine herself experiencing. She glanced at Ben in the chair beside her. At the head of the table, the attorney waited patiently for Loretta to arrive. He had worked quickly and efficiently. It had only been two days since her sister had agreed to this arrangement. She glanced at the still-empty chair. Provided Loretta hadn't changed her mind and left town.

Olivia's tension eased as the door opened and Loretta walked in alone. She took her seat and looked at the attorney. "Let's get this over and done. I have places to go."

"Where's your attorney?" Her sister looked at her with a blank expression.

"I don't need one."

Olivia's stomach knotted at the dispassionate tone in her sister's voice. She was giving up her child and all she could think about was getting away.

Mr. Freeman exchanged looks with Ben then proceeded. "Very well, let me explain the key points before you sign."

Olivia watched her sister as the attorney outlined the pertinent points, hoping for any sign of regret or doubt, but Loretta barely paid attention. She never dreamed her sister could be so callous. A new thought surfaced. Maybe it was harder than she'd expected and her desire to get away was more emotional than self-centered.

In a matter of moments, Olivia was signing the document, aware of her sister's scrawled signature above hers. Loretta pushed upright and picked up her purse.

"He's all yours now." She walked around the table and out the door.

Olivia watched her leave with a heavy heart. "Loretta." She hurried after her sister, and caught up with her in the hallway. "I know this has been hard for you, and I want you to know that I'd never keep Charlie from seeing you. You will always be welcome. You can visit him whenever you want."

Loretta held her gaze a moment. "Yeah. I know, but my life will be easier now."

If only there was something Olivia could say to let her sister know despite it all she still cared for her. "I can't help thinking that you might regret this one day."

"You changing your mind?"

"No. He'll be better off with me." She almost said *and Ben*. "He'll be happy here."

"And so will I. I can find my Mr. Right."

Olivia's hope for her sister crumbled. "Loretta, haven't you realized that no man can make you happy? You have to be happy with yourself first. You can't pin all your hopes on one human being because no man will be rich enough to satisfy what you're searching for."

Loretta looked her up and down with a disgusted expression. "Oh, I get it. Miss Goody Two Shoes wants me to be like her. Following the rules, on the straight and narrow, marrying some boring man who works eight to five and comes home to pot roast. Not for me. I want excitement and adventure. I like the unexpected, the impulsive."

Olivia's anger stirred even as she ached for her sister. "If being in a loving relationship, having a family and being at peace every day is being a Goody Two Shoes, then that's what I am." She took her sister's wrist. "You need more, something greater."

Loretta rolled her eyes. "Let me guess. Like an invisible God who only helps when He feels like it? Why didn't He help us by giving us good parents? Why did He give us a screwed-up mother and an absent father?"

Olivia sighed. "I don't know. I don't have all the answers."

"You can believe as you please, little sis, but I know that the right guy is out there for me, and I'll find him. You wait and see."

Olivia watched her sister disappear down the hall, wondering if she or Charlie would ever see her again. She'd pray for Loretta, that she'd come to see she needed the Lord in her life, not a wealthy, fallible human being.

Ben was struggling to determine Livvy's mood. She'd been silent since leaving the attorney's office. He supposed gaining custody of Charlie by taking him from his mother wasn't an easy thing to process. He had to admit to torn emotions himself.

He was relieved and overjoyed that the little guy wouldn't have to be taken from a home where he was loved and adored.

Now he had to tell Livvy that he was leaving town the day after tomorrow. He'd promised her he would give her warning the next time he went away. He had to tell her about his career goal, but how would she take the news that he was going to attend seminary?

He admitted to being a coward on this point. Revealing his faith had cost him his family, with the exception of Jeff. It had cost him the affection of a woman he was falling in love with. She had ended their relationship when he told her about his future plans. She wasn't about to be married to a man with no money and no future.

Logically, he doubted Olivia would react badly to his revelation, but she wouldn't be happy that he hadn't told her sooner. She'd probably consider it withholding important information and not being completely truthful, both of which would be black marks against him in her book. Jeff was right on this point. He may have waited too long and only caused more animosity and distrust.

He followed Livvy into her house. Her mood lifted suddenly. She turned and smiled. "Charlie is mine. He's going to be here with me from now on and I don't have to worry about his being taken away." She stepped toward him and placed her hands on his chest.

"Let's go get him at Nora's and tell him the news. I want to see his face."

Ben took her wrists in his hands. "Not just yet. I need to talk to you first." He motioned for her to take a seat. Settled on the sofa, he searched for a place to begin but found none. "Livvy, I'm leaving town soon. I'm moving up to Jackson."

The shock and confusion in her eyes lanced through him.

"Why? I don't understand. Did you get a job up there?"

"In a way. I'm going back to school to get a degree."

"School? For photography?"

"No. You see, I've been meeting with Pastor Shields because he's going to sponsor me for the program."

Olivia leaned away from him, then stood. "So you're leaving, going to school two hours away and you didn't bother to warn me, to let me know your plans?"

Ben rubbed his temple. "There's been a lot going on lately and…"

"How long have you known you'd be leaving?"

His throat clogged. "Since I first came here." Her eyes narrowed and darkened.

"I see. Well, I'm not surprised. I've been

expecting this. You have a habit of walking away when you're bored."

"You don't understand. I want to explain…"

She held up her hand. "No need. You came to make peace. We've done that and you're forgiven. Time for us to move on with our lives. We both knew your job was short-term. The bicentennial is over. You're free to go where you please. It's fine. We have no future, Ben. We both know that. Charlie was the only thing holding us together anyway."

A cold chill chased through his veins. He'd expected her to be upset, but he never expected her to say she didn't care. "So you're saying there's nothing between us. You have no feelings for me at all?"

She crossed her arms over her chest. "I told you from the beginning we could never be together again. That ended a long time ago. What you destroyed can't be repaired."

He saw tears in her eyes before she turned away. He knew she loved him; why was she doing this? Trust. Nora had warned him it would take time and superhuman patience. He'd done everything he could to regain her trust but it wasn't enough. Especially now that he'd kept his future plans from her. In her eyes, he hadn't changed at all.

"Livvy, please let me explain. I want you to believe when I tell you…"

She whirled around and faced him, her expression stoic. "Just go, Ben. Get your degree. I wish you all the best. Really."

"What about Charlie? I'll want to come and see him."

"Fine, we'll work something out for you two to spend time together."

Her message was clear. He could see Charlie but she wasn't part of the deal. His worst fear had been realized. Olivia had rejected him.

He turned and walked to the door, looking over his shoulder one last time. How could he have been so wrong? Nora warned him it would be hard to regain Olivia's trust. He'd give her room for now, but he had permission to come and visit Charlie. She may be cutting him out of her life, but he wasn't about to stop trying to win her back. Even if it took a lifetime. He'd give it some time, then he'd try explaining it to her again.

And again, if necessary.

Olivia sat on the back steps watching Charlie scale the small climbing wall on his new play set. They'd finished installing it this morning and Charlie had been over every inch from the swing and slide to the fort and ladder and the monkey bars on the side. She had alternated between delight and terror of the things he attempted.

He had some growing to do to fully enjoy the play equipment, but she looked forward to every new accomplishment. She'd installed a fence around the yard to keep him and Rudy safe, but each day she realized she couldn't keep him safe from everything. Those were the moments she missed Ben the most. It would have been comforting to have his sound perspective on things. And to share all the fun moments and cute things her nephew, her boy, would say and do.

He'd been gone now nearly two weeks, and no matter how hard she tried, she couldn't ignore the hollow inside her chest that even sweet Charlie couldn't fill. She enjoyed being a full-time mom but she'd have to find a job soon. She was still waiting on word from the city about the job as town manager. The powers that be were taking an unusually long time making up their minds. If she didn't get the job, then she'd have to start looking for something else, but the thought of leaving Charlie every day was depressing. Thankfully, Nora was still eager to watch him and Rudy.

Olivia had just finished feeding Charlie

lunch when Delores called, her voice filled with excitement. "I have some good news and an announcement."

Olivia smiled. It must be big for her boss to be so excited. The woman rarely showed her emotions. "What's happened?"

"The city council has decided to change the position of town manager to director of Main Street. It'll be more like a chamber of commerce job only it will focus on the businesses on the square and keeping events and activities organized."

"Oh. I guess that makes sense." It was a huge change from the mainly administrative town manager position.

"Olivia, they've asked me to take the job."

Her heart sank. She'd counted on getting the job, though she really wasn't all that disappointed it went to Delores. Besides, she could always go back to accounting. "Congratulations, Delores. I know you'll do a great job."

"I'm really excited about it. We'll be creating the job as we go along. You and I."

It took Olivia a moment for her words to register. "What do you mean?"

"I need an assistant and I want you to come to work as my right-hand man. We work well together and I know you'll be a huge asset to the town. What do you say?"

It was the perfect solution. She never liked being the boss; she was always happier as the sidekick. "I say yes. When do we start?"

"Bright and early Monday morning. We're going to be working out of our old bicentennial space so we don't even have to move."

Olivia's spirits soared in the clouds for the rest of the day. With the exception of those moments when something would remind her of Ben. Seeing Nora coming up the walk later that day was one of those moments. Nora always sent her thoughts spinning. Had she heard from Ben? Had something happened to him? Was he all right?

She greeted the older woman with a hug. "Charlie will be glad to see you. Let's sit out back and you can watch him on his new play set." She gauged the woman's attitude. "Everything all right?"

Nora smiled and nodded. "Right as rain."

After a detailed explanation from Charlie about all the marvels of his playground, Nora sat on the back porch with Olivia. "He's happier than I've ever seen him. But he asked me about Ben."

Olivia nodded. "He asks me too." She

wanted to ask about him herself but couldn't form the words.

"He misses you both." Nora glanced at her. "Thankfully he has his studies to occupy his mind."

Olivia searched her mind for something to say.

"Frankly, Olivia, I'm really surprised at your lack of support for his career. I never thought you'd turn him away because of his calling."

Olivia jerked her head toward her friend. "Calling? What are you talking about?"

Nora's eyes narrowed and she held her gaze a long time. "His entering the ministry."

"I don't know what you're talking about. I thought he was going back to school to get some degree."

"A theology degree. You mean he didn't tell you?"

Olivia shook her head, her mind replaying the events the last time she saw him. The truth twisted her lungs. "Oh, Nora, I didn't give him a chance. I heard him say he was leaving town and I shut down. I'd been waiting for that to happen. I assumed he had done what he'd come for and now he was moving on."

She pressed her hand against the side of her

face. "I told him I didn't love him, not in so many words, but I made it clear there could never be any relationship between us again."

"Oh, Olivia. I wondered what had happened. He was so down when he left. I was worried that he'd fallen into that black hole again."

"Why didn't he tell me?"

"You really don't know?" Nora took a deep breath. "When Ben came home from overseas he told his family that he'd become a Christian and they basically disowned him. All but his brother Jeff. His dad is an avowed atheist, and his mother is a new age religion junky. They saw his faith as a rejection of them and what they believe in. When he told them he wanted to become a minister they were furious. My brother, his dad, told him to never contact him again."

Olivia's heart ached. "That's why he needed a job. But I wouldn't have reacted that way. I can see it all so clearly now. Ben would be an amazing pastor."

"I believe so too but his former girlfriend walked out on him when he told her. She didn't see herself being poor and catering to a bunch of narrow-minded losers."

"Oh, no. So he was afraid I'd react the same way? He should have known better."

"Yes, but the woman he loved had just told him she didn't love him."

The pieces all fell into place with a snap. "Oh, Nora, I've been such a fool. And a coward. I was afraid to trust Ben again, but I realize now that I've trusted him for a long time. Marcy Jo told me I was holding a grudge and she was right. Not just against Ben but against God too. On some level I still blamed Him for the failed wedding." She shook her head. "My friend also told me to uncover the real issues I had."

"Did you?"

Olivia nodded and wiped moisture from her lashes. "I was nine when my parents split. I adored my father. He was kind and funny and I never doubted he loved me. He came into our bedroom one night. Loretta was already asleep. He came and kissed me good-night and told me he loved me. The next morning he was gone and I never saw or heard from him again."

"What did your mom say?"

"That he was gone, and I should forget about him."

Nora's gaze was filled with sympathy and understanding. She took her hand. "I'm so sorry."

"I think I've always been poised for people

leaving. Then Ben didn't show up and when Charlie was taken, it just confirmed what my mother always told us. Never trust a man." She met Nora's gaze. "But she was wrong. I was wrong."

"Yes, she was. Especially where Ben is concerned."

She wiped tears from her eyes. "Nora, I've got to make this right. Where is he?"

"At a seminary in Jackson. I can give you his number."

Olivia nodded, her mind already making plans. "But I don't want to call him. This has to be done in person." She stood and called to Charlie. "Do you want to go see Big Ben?"

Charlie grinned and nodded then jumped off the fort and ran toward her. She gathered him up in her arms. "Can Rudy come too? He's misses Big Ben a whole lot."

"Sure. He's part of the family."

"When are we going?"

"Right now. Get Rudy's leash."

Charlie whooped and jumped up and down then dashed into the house, returning with the red leash. "Come on, Mommy. We have to hurry. Big Ben is sad without us."

Olivia exchanged looks with Nora, who was smiling and nodding her approval.

Charlie asked about Ben every mile on the

way to Jackson, making the two-hour trip seem twice as long, but it didn't matter. All Olivia could think of was finding Ben and telling him she loved him and she wanted to spend her life with him.

Olivia pulled to a stop near the campus library. Nora had checked Ben's schedule and told her he should be there now. She suddenly saw a flaw in her plan. She couldn't simply walk into the library and start shouting for Ben and she couldn't take Rudy inside. She didn't want to text him either. She had it in her mind to completely surprise him.

Unfastening Charlie from his car seat, she decided to go sit on the bench she saw in the grassy area outside the building and figure out what to do next. Besides, Charlie and Rudy needed to work off some energy.

After about ten minutes, she settled on texting Ben and not worrying about the surprise aspect when a young man strolled by, obviously on his way to the library.

"Excuse me."

He stopped and smiled. "Can I help you?"

"Do you know Ben Kincaid?"

"No. Can't say I do but this is a big place."

She nodded. She'd never been to a seminary before, but this campus was huge and sprawling. "He's supposed to be inside the library, but I can't take the dog. Could you see if he's there? He's in his early thirties, about six feet two, light brown hair, blue eyes. Oh, and he has dimples."

She blushed when she realized her voice had taken on a dreamy tone.

The young man grinned. "I'll see if I can find him."

Seated back on the bench, she watched Charlie running around and questioned her impulsive plan. Maybe she should just call him and say *I'm here* and then...

"Big Ben!" Charlie yelped and ran toward the building. Olivia stood and saw Ben trotting down the steps then breaking into a jog as he realized Charlie was rushing toward him. Her heart turned to mush as she watched the big man scoop up the little boy and hold him tightly against his chest.

His gaze found hers and he started forward. She didn't realize she'd begun moving until he was close enough to touch. The love she saw in his blue eyes sent her pulse racing. Rudy greeted Ben by putting his paws on Ben's legs.

"Livvy, what are you doing here? The guy said my family was outside waiting to see me."

Charlie answered for her. "We came to see you. We missed you. Didn't we, Mommy?"

Ben kissed the boy's cheek. "I've missed you too, little buddy." He looked at her, eyebrows arched. "Mommy?"

"He just started calling me that. I didn't have a problem with it."

"Rudy is glad to see you, Big Ben."

Ben held her gaze, puzzlement reflected in his eyes.

Olivia took his hand. "We're your family and we came to tell you we love you."

"We?"

"I love you, Ben. I always have. That day you told me you were leaving I reacted out of fear. I'd been waiting for you to walk away from the moment you returned. I didn't give you a chance to explain because I was so hurt and angry. It was like you were disappearing all over again. All I could think of was to push you away."

"What changed?"

"Nora told me where you were, what your future plan was." She stepped close. "She also told me how your parents and your friend reacted. I'm so sorry. But how could you think I'd be like them?"

"I didn't, but when you told me you had no feelings for me…" He shrugged. "I assumed the worst. You sounded like you were good with me leaving. I thought I misread everything."

She reached up and touched his cheek. "Then let me tell you right now that I'd be proud and honored to be a pastor's wife."

Ben set Charlie on the ground and pulled her into his arms. "I never dreamed you could ever forgive me or love me."

"We've both changed, Ben, grown up. I think maybe it's time to arrange a new wedding."

He pulled her close and spoke softly in her ear. "Whatever you want. Cake, flowers, ribbons, I'll pay attention to every detail. I promise."

She chuckled. "This time I want small, simple and personal. No frills. Just us."

Olivia melted into his kiss, losing track of time. She became aware of voices and a low whistle. They separated to see the sidewalk filling with students. She saw Ben's cheeks redden and felt her own grow warm. She bit her lip and smiled. "I guess we should take this someplace more private."

"I've got to go to class, but it's Friday so I'll head back to Blessing tonight, and we can resume our…conversation then."

The smile he gave her left no doubt where his heart was.

"I'll fix your favorite meal and we can make plans."

Ben kissed her briefly then picked up Charlie and held them both close. "I don't care what we eat as long as we're together. A family."

Epilogue

❧

One month later

Olivia buttoned Charlie's little suit jacket, then tugged in place and straightened the tiny tie. "You look so handsome." The boy grinned and glanced at his dog, who was sitting patiently nearby. "Does Rudy look handsome too?"

Olivia smiled. The animal was sporting a bow tie around his neck and looking very dapper. "Yes, he does." Her heart was so full of love and thankfulness it couldn't hold another ounce.

Today was her wedding day. In a short while she and Ben would be husband and wife. They'd taken a long and difficult road to reach this point, but she knew going forward, no matter what life tossed their way, they would tackle it as a team. Together. The three of them.

She smoothed Charlie's hair and gave him a kiss.

"Can I go see Big Ben and show him we match? Can I call him Daddy now?"

She and Marcy Jo chuckled. "No, not yet. We have to go down the aisle and see Pastor Shields. He'll say some words then Big Ben and I will kiss and then he'll be your daddy." No reason to try and explain to the boy about legal adoption. As far as the three of them were concerned, once they said their vows, they would be a family.

She glanced at Marcy Jo. "Can you take him to Ben? I'll be ready in about five minutes."

Charlie gave Olivia a serious look. "Is a wedding like a birthday party?"

"Not in the beginning. It's serious but afterward we'll have a party at Aunt Nora's house."

"With cake?"

"Yes, cake and lots of other yummy goodies."

"Cool." He took Marcy Jo's hand. "Mommy, you look pretty."

"Thank you, sweetheart." Olivia clasped her hands to her heart. Whatever dreams she'd had for the first wedding, they paled in light of the joy and perfection of this one.

Stepping to the mirror she made one last survey. No white gown this time, only an unadorned white dress that skimmed her calves and had a bodice that was simple and elegant.

They'd decided to be married in Ben's church with Pastor Shields officiating and only close friends and family in attendance. Marcy Jo, Delores, Jeff and Nora. They would have a small reception at Nora's after the ceremony.

Olivia picked up her bouquet. Ben had offered to replicate her first one again, but she'd declined. Together they had decided on a different arrangement. White roses for her, daisies for Charlie and ivy for Ben. They'd planned a honeymoon at the beach with Charlie and Rudy. They'd take a trip together later when Ben had a break in school.

Marcy Jo returned and started fussing with Olivia's dress. "You look beautiful. Have you and Ben decided where to live? Are you moving to Jackson?"

"No. Charlie and I will stay here while he's in school. He's only two hours away so he'll come home as often as he can."

"And when he's a full-fledged minister?"

Olivia touched the necklace Ben had given

her last night. A small Blessing Bridge on a delicate platinum chain. "We'll go wherever the Lord needs us."

Marcy Jo gave her a hug. "Are you ready?"

Olivia sighed and grinned. "So ready."

She stepped to the end of the aisle and saw Ben, Charlie and Rudy all waiting. Her gaze found Ben's and her heart flipped over. This was the moment she'd thought of so many times. The one she'd seen in her mind's eye that had never taken place.

But it would today. Ben was waiting for her, tall, handsome and in his tux.

The music started and she took her first step toward her dream.

"Thank You, Lord, for Your perfect timing."

* * * * *

Dear Reader,

Writers are always asking—What if? So I had wondered for a long time what if a jilted bride met up with the groom again. Could they ever start again? That was the idea behind Ben and Olivia's story and it proved to be a challenge.

Where do you begin to forgive someone who shattered your lifelong dreams and left you alone at the altar? And what about the groom? Did he have any remorse or regrets? How had they changed in the time apart? One rule of life applied here—people won't change unless they are forced to.

Both Ben and Olivia have changed since the failed wedding day; they grew up and now see the world through a different lens. There is plenty of forgiveness needed on all fronts. Ben has to deal with his past mistakes and failures, and Olivia has to deal with her pain and humiliation, but also the addition of her nephew that shakes up her life.

We never know what life will toss at us from one day to the next. Change is always unexpected. How we deal with those sudden shifts reveals our character. Ben and Olivia both need to draw on their faith and trust in the Lord to meet each turn in their lives. But the scars of the past make it difficult. Truth and trust both have to be part of a relationship, and until those are addressed head-on, there can be no future.

It takes the loss of something precious to both of them before they can break down the last barriers and make a life together. I hope you enjoy their reunion romance as much as I did writing it.

Lorraine